THE PUFFIN TREASURY OF

MODERN INDIAN STORIES

This book belongs to

Anant Tikke

THE PUFFIN TREASURY OF

MODERN INDIAN STORIES

edited by mala dayal

PUFFIN BOOKS

For Ravi, mentor and favourite editor

PUFFIN BOOKS

Penguin Books India (P) Ltd., 11 Community Centre, Panchsheel Park, New Delhi 110 017, India
Penguin Books Ltd., 80 Strand, London WC2R 0RL
Penguin Putnam Inc., 375 Hudson Street, New York, NY 10014, USA
Penguin Books Australia Ltd., 250 Camberwell Road, Camberwell, Victoria 3124, Australia
Penguin Books Canada Ltd., 10 Alcorn Avenue, Suite 300, Toronto, Ontario, M4V 3B2, Canada
Penguin Books (NZ) Ltd., Cnr Rosedale & Airborne Roads, Albany, Auckland, New Zealand

First published in Puffin by Penguin Books India 2002

This anthology copyright © Penguin Books India 2002
Introduction copyright © Mala Dayal 2002
Illustrations copyright © Penguin Books India 2002
The copyright for the individual pieces vests with the authors or their estates
Page vii is an extension of the copyright page

All rights reserved

10 9 8 7 6 5 4 3 2 1

Printed at Tien Wah Press, Singapore

CONTENTS

ACKNOWLEDGEMENTS

I sought the advice of many friends when compiling this volume. Special thanks are due to Arvind Gupta, Paro Anand and Monisha Mukundan. Mahasweta Devi generously allowed me to include 'The Why-Why Girl' which forms part of my Introduction.

—Editor

✳ ✳ ✳

The editor and publishers gratefully acknowledge the following for permission to reproduce copyright pieces in this anthology:

Paro Anand: 'Shadow' from *Impossible: Tales of the Unknown* (Rupa & Co, 2002) © Paro Anand, reprinted by permission of the publisher; **Margaret Bhatty**: 'The Magic of the Red and Gold Shoe' (first published by UNESCO, *Stories from Asia 2*, Tokyo, 1984) © Margaret Bhatty, reprinted by permission of Margaret Bhatty; **Pankaj Bisht**: from *Bholu and Golu* (National Book Trust, India, 1996) English translation © National Book Trust, India, reprinted by permission of the publisher; **Ruskin Bond**: 'Snake Trouble' (National Book Trust, India, 1991) © Ruskin Bond, reprinted by permission of the publisher; **Anita Desai**: 'Games at Twilight' © Anita Desai, reprinted by permission of Anita Desai; **Shashi Deshpande**: from *The Narayanpur Incident* (Penguin Books India, 1995) © Shashi Deshpande, reprinted by permission of Shashi Deshpande; **Mahasweta Devi**: 'The Why-Why Girl' © Mahasweta Devi, printed by permission of Mahasweta Devi; **Shama Futehally**: 'The Tunnel' from *Sorry, Best Friend!* edited by Githa Hariharan and Shama Futehally (Tulika, Chennai, 1997) © Shama Futehally, reprinted by permission of the publisher; **Mala Marwah**: 'Bidesia Babu' (first published in *Apna Express, Indian Express*, Delhi, 1990) © Mala Marwah, reprinted by permission of Mala Marwah; **R.K. Narayan**: 'Granny Shows Her Ignorance' from *Swami and Friends* (Hamish Hamilton, 1935) © the Estate of R.K. Narayan, reprinted by permission of the author's Estate; **Premchand**: 'Festival of Eid' (National Book Trust, India, 1980) © Amrit Rai, reprinted by permission of the publisher; **Shanta Rameshwar Rao**: 'The Concert' © Shanta Rameshwar Rao, printed by permission of Shanta Rameshwar Rao; **Hemangini Ranade**: 'Sorry, Best Friend!' from *Sorry, Best Friend!* edited by Githa Hariharan and Shama Futehally (Tulika, Chennai, 1997) © Hemangini Ranade, reprinted by permission of the publisher; **Satyajit Ray**: 'The Hungry Septopus' from *The Best Thirteen: A Collection of the Best Stories from 13 Languages of India* (National Book Trust, India, 2000) © The Estate of Satyajit Ray, reprinted by permission of the publisher; **Salman Rushdie**: from *Haroun and the Sea of Stories* (Granta/Penguin UK, 1990) © Salman Rushdie, reprinted by permission of the publisher; **Bhisham Sahni**: 'The Boy with a Catapult' from *The Best Thirteen: A Collection of the Best Stories from 13 Languages of India* (National Book Trust, India, 2000) © Bhisham Sahni, reprinted by permission of the publisher; **Subhadra Sen Gupta**: 'Dal Delight' from *History, Mystery Dal and Biryani: Stories of the Past* (Scholastic India Pvt. Ltd., 2000) © Subhadra Sen Gupta, reprinted by permission of the publisher; **Poile Sengupta**: 'The Lights Changed' from *Sorry, Best Friend!* edited by Githa Hariharan and Shama Futehally (Tulika, Chennai, 1997) © Poile Sengupta, reprinted by permission of the publishers; **Vikram Seth**: 'The Elephant and the Tragopan' from *Beastly Tales from Here and There* (Penguin Books India, 1992) © Vikram Seth, reprinted by permission of Vikram Seth; **Kalpana Swaminathan**: from *The True Adventures of Prince Teentang* (HarperCollins India, 1993) © Kalpana Swaminathan, reprinted by permission of the publishers.

INTRODUCTION

An introduction to an anthology of stories for children, broadly between the ages of eight and twelve, is perhaps dispensable as it is unlikely to be read by them. Nevertheless, some explanation for the selection in this volume seems necessary. Unlike literature for children in many countries, in India there is very little material specifically designed for them which has delighted successive generations and is also enjoyed by children today. Here, stories that have gone down from grandparent to parent to child are mostly from the Epics, myths, legends and folktales, the *Panchatantra, Jatakas, Kathasaritsagara* and the *Hitopadesha*. So instead of taking excerpts, most of the stories in this volume stand on their own: only a few have been extracted from novels of well-known writers like R.K. Narayan's *Swami and Friends*, Salman Rushdie's *Haroun and the Sea of Stories*, and Dhan Gopal Mukerji's *Gay-Neck: The Story of a Pigeon*.

The main aim of *The Puffin Treasury of Modern Indian Stories* is to offer some of the best Indian children's fiction available in English. All the authors included are renowned storytellers whose imagination, skill, elegant prose and wit have won them acclaim and awards. They have also given us stories for children which will endure for times to come.

A few translations are included. Very little children's fiction from the Indian languages has been rendered into English. Of the published material, good translations are hard to come by.

I have also done my best to include as wide a range of themes as I could. So we have a ghost story, fantasies, humour, historical fiction, real-life incidents, those that sensitively explore the inner world of the child, the serious, the light-hearted and the whimsical.

The book is profusely illustrated by some of India's most talented artists, who have complemented and enlivened the twenty-one selected works. As the stories showcase the best of English fiction for children in India, the illustrations showcase the skill and versatility of Indian illustrators.

Poverty, inequality, communal tension, degradation of the environment confront today's children. This collection also reflects these concerns, deftly and subtly. Faced with a complex environment, the Indian child cannot be a passive observer but is constantly questioning. I conclude this Introduction with one of my favourite pieces written by Mahasweta Devi when she was sitting across the table in my room: 'The Why-Why Girl'. Even if children are reluctant readers of introductions, I am sure that those who have got thus far will relish our why-why girl.

Mala Dayal
New Delhi 2002

THE WHY-WHY GIRL

Mahasweta Devi

'But why?'

The girl was small, about ten years old. She was chasing a large snake. I ran after her, dragged her back by her pigtails and shouted, 'No, Moina, no!'

'Why?' she asked.

'It's not a grass snake nor a rat snake. It's a cobra.'

'Why shouldn't I catch a cobra?'

'Why should you?'

'We eat snakes, you know. The head you chop off, the skin you sell, the meat you cook.'

'Not this time.'

'I will. I will.'

'No child!'

'But why?'

I dragged her back to the Samiti office where Moina's mother, Khiri, was weaving a basket. 'Come, rest a little,' I said.

'Why?'

'Why not? Aren't you tired?'

Moina shook her head. 'Who will bring the Babu's goats home? And collect firewood and fetch water and lay the trap for the birds?'

Khiri said, 'Don't forget to thank the Babu for the rice he sent.'

'Why? Didn't I have to sweep the cowshed and do a thousand jobs for him? Did he thank me? Why should I thank him?'

Moina ran off. Khiri shook her head. 'Never saw a child like this. All she keeps saying is "why". The village postmaster calls her the "Why-why girl".'

'I like her.'

'She's so obstinate and unyielding.'

Moina was a Sabar, and the Sabars were poor and landless. But the other Sabars never complained. Only Moina's questions were endless.

'Why do I have to walk miles to the river for water? Why do we live in a leaf hut? Why can't we eat rice twice a day?'

Moina was the goatherd of the village Babus, but she was neither humble nor grateful to her employers. She did her work and came home, muttering, 'Why should I eat their leftovers? I will cook a delicious meal with green leaves and rice and crabs and chilli powder in the evening and eat with the family.'

The Sabars do not usually send their daughters to work. But Moina's mother was lame, her father had gone to faraway Jamshedpur in search of work and her brother, Goro, went to the forest to collect firewood. So Moina had to work.

That October I stayed at the Samiti for a month. One morning Moina declared that she would move into the Samiti hut with me.

Khiri said, 'You won't.'

'Why not? It's a big hut. How much space does one old woman need?'

'What about your work?'

'I'll come after work.'

And she came with one change of clothes and a baby mongoose. 'It eats very little and chases away the bad snakes,' she said. 'The good snakes I catch and give to mother. She makes lovely snake curry. I'll bring some for you.'

Malati Bonal, our Samiti teacher, told me, 'She'll exhaust you with her "whys".'

What a time I had that October! 'Why do I have to graze the Babu's goats? His boys can do it themselves. Why can't the fish speak? Why do the stars look so small if many of them are bigger than the sun?'

And every night, 'Why do you read books before you go to sleep?'

'Because books have the answers to your whys!'

For once Moina was silent. She tidied the room, watered the flowering rangan tree and gave fish to the mongoose. Then she said, 'I'll learn to read and get to know the answers to my questions.'

She would graze the goats and tell other children all she had learnt from me. 'Many stars are bigger than the sun. They live far away, so they look small. The sun is nearer, so it looks bigger…The fish do not speak like us. They have a fish language, which is silent…The earth is round, did you know that?'

When I went to the village a year later, the first thing I heard was Moina's voice. 'Why is the school closed?' she challenged Malati as she entered the Samiti school, dragging a bleating goat.

'What do you mean, "why"?'

'Why shouldn't I study too?'

'Who's stopping you?'

'But there's no class!'

'School is over.'

'Why?'

'You know, Moina, I take classes from 9 to 11 in the morning.'

Moina stamped her feet and said, 'Why can't you change the hours? I have to graze the Babu's goats in the morning. I can only come after eleven. If you don't teach, how will I learn? I will tell the old lady that none of us, goatherds and cowherds, can come if the hours are not changed.'

Then she saw me and fled with her goat.

I went to Moina's hut in the evening. Nestling close to the kitchen fire, Moina was telling her little sister and elder brother, 'You cut one tree and plant another two. You wash your hands before you eat, do you know why? You'll get stomach pain if you don't. You know nothing—do you know why? Because you don't attend Samiti classes.'

Who do you think was the first girl to be admitted to the village primary school?

Moina.

Moina is eighteen now. She teaches at the Samiti school. If you pass the school you're sure to hear her impatient, demanding voice, 'Don't be lazy. Ask me questions. Ask me why mosquitoes should be destroyed...Why the Pole Star is always in the north sky.'

And the other children, too, are learning to ask 'why'.

Moina doesn't know I'm writing her story. If told, she'd say, 'Why? Writing about me? Why?'

Illustrated by Ajanta Guhathakurta

Paro Anand

•

SHADOW

Prashant loved dogs. With all his heart. But there was one problem. His parents hated dogs. He tried to make them change their mind, begged and pleaded with them—even tried to blackmail them. But they were firm in their belief that dogs were dirty, disease-ridden, dangerous, disgusting, disruptive and downright doglike. Nothing that Prashant said or did would change their dogged attitude.

So Prashant did what he thought was the next best thing. He invented a dog. He made up a gorgeous cocker spaniel. Black. With soft silken ears. 'I'd like to have a bigger dog—a boxer, retriever or even a Great Dane,' thought Prashant. But then he decided to be sensible. 'Big dogs eat a lot, are difficult to hide from parents' prying eyes.' So, a black cocker spaniel it was. Silk-furred, liquid-eyed and silent. Silent as a shadow slipping past all disapproval. So he called him Shadow. Also because he shadowed him everywhere— to school, to tuition and to bed. Shadow never left his side, and he always reached down to pat Shadow's tufted head to reassure him that all was right with the world just as long as they were together.

Prashant grew to love Shadow very

much. As if he were a real dog. And he became very real to him. Prashant now started to feed his pup—stealing bread, milk and bones from the kitchen when no one was about. He had bought a plastic bowl which he filled twice a day with goodies. At first, of course, he also had to flush the soggy milk-soaked bread down the loo, and it was often stale and sour and made his mother yell at him about keeping his room clean. Luckily, she believed in him doing his own work, so she never discovered the source of the smell.

But, one day, the milk and bread was gone when Prashant went to clean the bowl! 'Good boy, Shadow,' he whispered. After that the bowl was regularly licked clean.

'Do you notice a change in the boy?' asked his father.

'Yes,' said his mother, 'he seems happier. I'm glad.'

'I think he's too much of a dreamer,' said the father, disapprovingly.

'Oh it's just a stage,' reassured the mother. 'At least he's stopped that nonsense about wanting a dog.'

Prashant was indeed happier. But he also became more secretive, spending more and more time on his own. Alone in his bedroom. His mother began to worry and talked to her sister who pronounced the dreaded words, 'Drug', ominously. Promptly Prashant was packed off to the doctor. But, of course, he was clean of anything like that.

'Do you think your parents are good to you?'

'Of course, doctor.'

'Are they fair to you?'

'Y—yes.'

'Is there anything you feel they've denied unfairly?'

'Well,' said Prashant. 'I always wanted a dog. Really, really badly. But they won't allow me to have one. But that's okay now.'

'So they got you a dog?'

'No, but I don't want one. Now.'

'Why not?'

'Because...' And he almost told the doctor about Shadow. But luckily he didn't. They'd have him in the looney bin if he confessed to playing with an imaginary dog. Only Prashant knew that Shadow wasn't imaginary. After all, he ate the food that Prashant put for him, didn't he?

'Nothing,' he replied, and no amount of coaxing would get him to break his sullen silence. 'A holiday might do him good' was the best the doctor could finally suggest.

So Bombay it was, where Prashant had three cousins, Ashish, Ashwin and Ashim. 'Boys who behave as boys should,' said his father.

Prashant secretly packed Shadow's bowl and assured him that an overnight journey by Rajdhani wouldn't be too bad. Shadow was nervy nevertheless and snuggled close to him on the upper berth, where they rocked into eventual sleep.

The next morning, Prashant had little black hairs stuck to him. 'Poor quality blankets on the railway,' complained his mother as she dusted them off. Prashant's back was turned to her so she didn't see him grin at the empty berth overhead.

Prashant settled easily into his new routine. He awoke at the crack of dawn and went with his cousins to the beach and swam for an hour before the crowds came. Then home for a huge breakfast. Then holiday homework kept them busy till lunch. Then it was cricket or lolling or something before going for another walk or swim, then TV and bed. His parents were delighted as he tanned and muscled his way to better health. For Prashant there was just one problem. He shared Ashwin's bedroom. He had to be very careful when feeding Shadow. He did not want to be caught in the act. And Shadow was as good as gold and as quiet as the proverbial mouse. Prashant had tried several times to persuade him to come for a swim, but Shadow was nervous

about the huge expanse of water and made it clear that he preferred the safety of the bedroom.

The trouble arose when Ashish, the eldest, two years Prashant's senior, began to brag about his swimming prowess. True, Ashish was bigger and brawnier than him, but Prashant couldn't bear being belittled like this. Recklessly, one morning he challenged Ashish to a race. They agreed that there would be two races, one 100 m or so—the distance was measured by two rocks which stood roughly 100 m apart, the other long distance—you had to swim as far out as you could, or dared.

'Wish you'd come to see me, Shadow, I'm going to show that big mouth a thing or two.' But Shadow politely declined by snuggling further into the bed.

'Ashwin, wake up...,' whispered Prashant.

'Oh yaar, I'm not coming. I watched TV till pretty late last night. I'm going to sleep on.'

Prashant shrugged and slipped into his trunks. 'Bye, Shadow...lick me luck!'

'What're you talking to your pillow for?' grumbled a sleepy Ashwin. Prashant nearly leapt out of his skin. 'Idiot!' he covered up. 'I was talking to you—wish me luck.'

'Oh,' replied Ashwin, sleepily. 'Well, best of luck and may the best nut win.'

Ashish was already near the gate with little Ashim by his side. Ashim was very excited about being judge. As they walked down to the beach, Ashim was the only one who spoke. 'The 100-m race will be swum first. I'll sit on Flat Rock, you start from Fat Rock. For the second race, you start at Flat Rock after a five-minute rest. You swim and see who runs out of stamina first. But remember, you have to swim back. Keep enough fuel for the return journey—there are no petrol pumps on the way! Heh heh!'

Putting their towels down, they waded out into the water. The horizon was a mauvy pink, calm and beautiful.

Prashant watched Ashim's hand go up and his voice came reedily over the breeze. 'On your marks—get set,' his arm had only just started to come down when Ashish shot out. 'Hey!' shouted Prashant in protest but then decided to try to catch up. Despite the poor start, Prashant pulled strongly and soon drew level with his cousin. He knew he had to get ahead for his opponent's arms were longer and would reach the finish line first even if they were head to head. Prashant surged forward at the very last second. He felt the flat firmness of the rock under his hand and knew that he had won. He came up grinning.

'Ashish wins!' yelled Ashim, leaping demonically on Flat Rock.

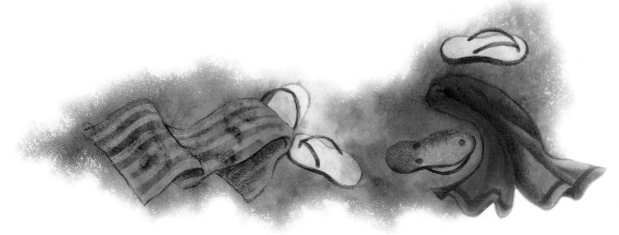

'WHAT?' yelled Prashant, 'What! Don't be an idiot, I won!'

'Don't be a bad loser, yaar. You lost, I won—that's that.'

'I didn't,' hissed Prashant. 'I didn't lose and you didn't win. This punk is a lying cheat.' Prashant was shaking with fury. He felt like hitting Ashish and pushing Ashim off his judge's throne.

'Okay, Champ. If you're so good, you can do it again. There's another race yet. You beat me this time.'

His taunting voice enraged Prashant further. 'I will,' he vowed. 'You lying cheat, I'll do it again. Only this time I'll swim so far out, there'll be no dispute.' He saw his cousins exchange an amused, conspiratorial look. He had to win. Just had to.

As Ashim yelled 'Go!' Prashant pushed away from the rock. He felt the ripples as Ashish surged ahead. 'Good, let him get ahead. This isn't about speed, it's distance,' thought Prashant, falling into a slow, steady rhythm. He let the warm silkiness of the water envelope and soothe him. Prashant swam further and further, on and on.

'Hey, Champ!' yelled Ashish, bringing him back to reality. 'Planning to turn back?' Prashant could make out by the raggedness of his voice that his opponent had begun to tire.

'No,' he replied and swam on, slow and steady. In the flush of unfair victory, Ashish had started out too strong. Too late he had realized his opponent's gambit. He realized that Prashant was good for another mile whereas he needed desperately to turn back. And, there was the return journey...

'Hey, Champ, let's agree to a draw and turn back,' he suggested. But Prashant pushed on, and Ashish fell behind.

'Okay, okay yaar, you've won. I admit it. Now let's turn back.'

The distance between them widened.

'Hey, you want to go the whole hog?—I agree, you won the 100 m too. I'd bribed Ashim to back me.'

His voice sounded faint now. 'Turn back, Prashant. I don't know what you're trying to prove.' Ashish had stopped and was treading water. He waited for Prashant to turn back. He didn't. Ashish yelled at him once more, urging him to come back. Then he shrugged a what-can-I-do shrug and turned back to the shore. His cousin was a tiny dot on the blue-brown water. 'Idiot!' he muttered as he headed homewards.

Prashant felt happy. He felt strong too. He had no intention of turning back. Suddenly the anger went out of him. He wondered why he'd been so fired up to win a silly race.

He just wanted to remain in the protective sheath of water. If only Shadow were with him. Shadow, his best friend, confidant. It was better than having a real dog who would lick everyone's hands, wag his tail at everyone. Shadow licked only his hand. He was his, only his.

Then the energy left him. It was sudden. Not a gradual tiring. Suddenly Prashant felt that he couldn't swim another stroke. He turned but all he could see was the sea all around. The shore was nowhere in sight. Growing panic and fear clouded his sense of direction. He pumped his legs to keep afloat, but the water seemed to reach up, pulling him in and under.

'Shadow!' he screamed. 'Shadow, Shadow help me!'

He sobbed as his arms and legs turned to lead and he felt the demons of the underworld suck him under. As he went down, he saw four black furry legs pumping the water furiously. It was Shadow. He had come to his rescue. 'Shadow!' he screamed, as water rushed into his mouth, choking him. And then he lost consciousness...

The fishermen found him, awash on the beach. His clothes had been torn by claws. 'Shadow...' the boy whispered as the water was forced out of his lungs. 'Shadow, where are you?' As they carried him to hospital, he mumbled, 'Shadow, where are you? Are you all right?' But he knew that he wasn't...he remembered the dog going down. Down into the terrible waves. 'Shadow...' he sobbed as they laid him on the white hospital bed.

His parents were summoned. 'He's all right but delirious,' the doctor pronounced. 'He's lucky, though, that his dog was there, or he may not have survived.'

'His dog? But, doctor, he doesn't have a dog.'

'Oh? Well, he says that his dog Shadow saved him. And there is no doubt about it. There are clear canine tooth and claw marks on your boy. Your boy was saved by a dog!'

Illustrated by Ajanta Guhathakurta

Margaret Bhatty

·

THE MAGIC OF THE RED AND GOLD SHOE

Lata was first at the water tap. She usually was because old Amma, her grandmother, went early to work in the homes of the rich beyond the railway station where she swept, scrubbed and swabbed. She would return at noon with leftovers of food for Lata; the red cock, Lalu; two hens; Maow, the tom cat; Rakhi, the goat; and Kalu, the black dog; and then go off again to do the evening chores.

Lata never lingered at the tap. And certainly not today—not when all the girls were talking about today's doll-marriage party. What will you wear? What are we getting to eat? Never before had a match been arranged more grandly. The plastic doll from the sweet seller's house was to be married to the rubber doll from the betel seller's. Anyone would be proud to get her doll married into the sweet seller's house, for it was the richest in the lane, and the feast would be something to talk about for days afterwards. There would doubtless be pieces of stale barfi from the sweet seller's own shop, fried crisps, rewari and maybe even buttermilk only a day old. Lata was never invited to any weddings. She was shabby, she had no father, her mother was dead, and her grandmother worked as a domestic servant. She couldn't provide a feast for the neighbourhood children because she lived on scraps off the tables of the rich.

When one is not invited to the most important function on one's street, just two doors away, there's no point standing around at the tap discussing it. So Lata hurried away as soon as her pot was full. She was never invited to any doll-marriage feast; but neither was she the only one. Six-year-old Joseph

Pinto never attended because he couldn't walk after polio had left his legs useless. He sat on his bed in his house most of the time except when Lata came, as she did today, and carried him out on her back, creeping through a hole in the railway fence to the green grass on the other side. Here she gently set him down while Rakhi the goat went off to graze.

Jumping off the embankment, Rakhi trotted along the tracks, her hoofs tapping on the cross-ties as she went. 'Rakhi! Come back!' Lata yelled. 'Isn't the grass good enough right here?' It never was, for a goat always sees finer patches farther ahead, and off she went. Rakhi was a city goat and knew how to look after herself.

The children's favourite place for playing was a hollow in the embankment where, seasons ago, mud had been dug out by men working on the line. The hollow was overgrown with short grass now, and Lata settled Joseph into it, drawing his legs out before him so that he could balance where he sat.

Leaning back, Joseph looked high into the sky where flights of snowy white egrets winged their way towards the lakes set in the rolling hills of the national park. Or he watched giant jet planes zoom over.

'When I grow up, I shall fly,' he always said, repeating it every day to make sure it would happen. Joseph planned to do everything that needed no legs. So he would fly like a jet plane or an egret. Or he would drive a train. Engine drivers didn't need legs, not with all those many wheels whirling so fast to carry them along.

Whenever a long-distance train

thundered down the track, they watched it go, their hearts beating fast with excitement and a little fear. It made the ground heave and shake, and, unable to contain themselves, Lata and Joseph yelled and shouted, waving madly at the startled faces of the passengers in the windows. As the train flew past, the invisible rush of its wings blew against their faces and lifted their hair. It was a thrilling moment but it never lasted long enough.

'When I grow up I shall be an engine-driver,' vowed Joseph breathlessly, not looking at his legs lying side by side like the limp broken wings of a bird.

'Of course you will!' cried Lata, still feeling her heart thudding. 'And will you wave to me as you go past?'

'I'll blow the whistle all the way through here and make Momin Sheikh's pigeons on the factory roof go straight up into the air with fright, and scatter the people in all directions, and shake old Amma's house so that she will shout: "It's that devil Joseph again! Nobody else takes a train through here like that! He would bring the roof down on a tired old woman's head, would he?"'

Joseph was not really a boaster. He needed to talk big sometimes because he felt so small and unimportant the rest of the time.

Lata laughed as she hopped first on one foot and then on the other. It wasn't only because of the train that she was feeling good. There was something else: she had a secret, and now that she had enjoyed it for long enough, she was going to tell it to Joseph.

Standing before him on the slope, she said, 'I have ten paise!'

'From where?' he cried in pleased surprise as she held up the coin.

'Amma gave it to me before she left for work.'

Here was wealth indeed! One whole ten-copper coin! And now came the sweet agony of trying to decide how to spend it in such a way that they wouldn't be sorry afterwards. It was terrible to have to say, 'Those peanuts were not so good, were they? We should have bought the candyfloss—one ball for you and one for me.' But then how to be absolutely sure? Candyfloss went much too fast, and it left only a little taste of sweetness behind. Puffed rice went further. And a twist of toffee pulled off the vendor's pole and shaped into a butterfly or a bird stuck to the teeth and went even further. While a lemon drop could last for days if you sucked it only now and then and kept it wrapped in a piece of paper in your pocket.

'What will you buy?' asked Joseph seriously, for he knew this problem called for much thought.

Lata was quite sure what she would do. 'We'll have a doll-marriage too, and we'll have a feast.' So what if they'd not been invited? A marriage and a feast of their own would make things equal. Well, almost equal—for it couldn't be much of a marriage when one had no dolls. The groom was the wooden handle of a chisel with the blade snapped off from Joseph's house, and the bride was the short stout stick with which Lata's grandmother beat clothes at the pond. Both stood stiffly side by side against the fence, with eyes, a nose, and a mouth put on with a charred stick. For ten paise the feast had to be modest indeed, with roasted chana served in silver cups made from paper out of empty cigarette boxes they found along the tracks.

They ate the chana slowly and very solemnly. It would not do to gobble them too fast, for once they were gone the feast would be over. Too soon would their pleasure become a thing of the past. Each chana had to be chewed and tasted to the fullest so that they could be remembered to the fullest.

'We won't tell anybody—not anybody,' said Lata, munching.

'No, we won't tell anybody,' Joseph repeated, nodding his head, for there is always a certain pride in the possession of a secret of one's very own. However, the real truth was that it hadn't been much of a marriage. The others would laugh out loud and that they could not have endured.

What with all the preparation—hunting for tinfoil, running to the station to buy the chana from the old man at the level crossing there, and setting up the bride and bridegroom—the children were unaware of how the time had passed until Lata heard her grandmother calling from the lane on the other side of the fence.

But where was the goat? 'Rakhi! Rakhi!' she cried, jumping to her feet.

'She was down that way,' Joseph said, pointing along the tracks as Lata set off.

If luck were something one could be sure of, there wouldn't be any fun to it. 'If Rakhi hadn't strayed so far that day, we would never have found the shoe,' Lata always said later, convinced it was all because of their good luck.

She was running along the tracks, not even looking down, when the gleam caught her eye. All crimson and gold, it flashed in the afternoon sun. And when she went over and picked it up, her eyes opened wide with astonishment and delight. A child's shoe—and what a shoe! Of soft red velvet it was, with a leather sole, and worked all over from end to end with gold thread. The toe tapered to a fine golden point and curved back on itself. What was more, it was brand new. Perhaps its pair lies somewhere close by, thought Lata, as she searched along the tracks and among the bushes. But she didn't find it. There was only one shoe. Nevertheless, when you have never owned a pair of shoes in all your life, even one is better than none.

There was nothing magical about the shoe. What magic can there be in a thing thrown out of the window of a passing train by a wilful spoilt child who should have known better? But then again, what is magic if it isn't marvel and change, and all the difference between the ordinary and the extraordinary?

The change began working from that very day. Now there is a way of wearing only one shoe so that nobody will suspect it is only half of a pair. Or better still, there is a way to make it *appear* that wearing only one is the most natural thing in the world, and the only reason why more people don't do it is because other shoes are made for walking. This shoe was not.

Every evening Lata carried little Joseph Pinto out to a stone bench in the nearby park where he could watch the others play. It isn't a park really—only a half-hearted attempt at a park in the open space behind the shanty town where the city ends and the countryside begins. The statue in the centre is of

the man who first had the idea and donated the piece of land. But he died soon after and the rest of the money was spent on this statue, while the park was left unfinished. He is a tall stout figure of a man standing on a platform and Momin Sheikh's pigeons, the sparrows, crows and other birds have made a sorry mess of him. He is surrounded by a dozen or more small concrete posts from which it was planned to sling heavy chains, but the money was used up and everyone lost interest in the scheme. Janak Seth, he is called, and the children have made up a song that they sing as they play a game of their own around him:

Janak Raja went to Dilli,
Brought back thirteen bowls of gold,
Thirteen bowls for thirteen children,
Some still hungry, some still cold.

The one who is chosen to be the raja climbs onto the platform and takes his place between the broad feet of Janak Seth, holding a long stick in his hand. The others skip around and sing the jingle. When the raja brings his stick down to strike the closest post, there is a scramble to get to any one of the posts surrounding the statue. There is much laughter and yelling, much shoving, pushing, and hair pulling along with wrenching at each other's clothes. Arguments often grow so bitter that some don't speak to each other for days afterwards because all those who don't get to a pillar and cling to it for dear life are declared 'out' by the raja. However, in the next general scramble they usually get right back into the game. And so it goes, endlessly.

Lata had never been chosen raja and so she naturally thought it was a silly game. 'It's the stupidest game I ever saw, and I refuse to play,' she said since she wasn't given any place in the playing of it. 'Yes,' echoed little Joseph, to whom all such games had to seem silly. 'It's the stupidest game I ever saw.' So the two of them always pretended to be more interested in watching the big boys playing marbles or gilli-danda.

That evening Lata sat with one leg neatly folded under her, while the other hung down wearing the red and gold shoe. She swung her leg back and forth so that she could see it flash out from the corner of her eye. And sometimes she held her leg stiffly out before her as if she'd forgotten to swing it back. As she had hoped, she soon had a small knot of children gaping at her where she sat, though she pretended not to notice them.

'Where did you get such a grand pair of shoes?' asked one of the children in astonishment.

Lata didn't answer or even turn her head from watching the game of gilli-danda; but she was aware that more children were running across to join the crowd. The sweet seller's daughter, who was then the raja, was left perched alone on Janak Seth's feet and feeling very annoyed about it. Finally, she climbed down and pushed her way through the others to stand before Lata and Joseph.

Where did you get them? Is it real gold—all that thread? Who gave them to you? For a while Lata enjoyed the sensation, and then she and Joseph looked at each other and smiled all over their faces, the way we do when we're very pleased about something and don't care who knows it.

'My grandmother bought them for me,' Lata said serenely, pulling her shabby skirt straight to make sure that the other foot was well hidden from view.

'My father could buy a dozen such shoes,' sniffed the sweet seller's girl.

'Perhaps,' Lata responded, 'but he hasn't done so yet, has he?'

She held out her foot, turning the ankle a bit to let them all get a good look. The shoe wasn't a good fit. In fact it hurt a bit—but for the sensation it was causing it was well worth a pinched toe or two.

'It's a beautiful pair of shoes,' someone breathed.

'But there's only one!' burst out the simple-hearted Joseph before Lata could stop him.

Only *one*? How silly! Only *one* shoe! Shoes always come in pairs, don't they?

'Yes, but this isn't for walking in. It's a shoe for show,' chattered Joseph, for all this sudden success had quite gone to his little head.

'Hear that!' sneered the sweet seller's daughter. 'Only *one* shoe, and that only for show! You should know all about that, O Legless One!'

Poor Joseph's face fell, for he always felt sensitive about his sorry legs.

'It is too!' cried Lata stoutly. 'It's not for walking. See?'

Slipping it off, she turned it over to show them the underside was still smooth and unsoiled. And inside there was a soft sole of grey felt. 'It's a shoe only for show.'

It certainly was, and she was not going to waste her time arguing with people who refused to believe the evidence of their eyes. 'Have you ever seen anyone walking in such shoes?' Along the dusty lanes of the shanty town? Through the slush by the water tap and the coal dust and the litter and the cattle droppings? Of course they hadn't!

They passed the shoe from hand to hand, and Lata watched jealously as they examined it.

'Can I try it on?' asked one of the girls, and Lata looked at her for a long moment. 'Only for a second—just to see what it feels like,' the girl pleaded.

This was something new indeed—to be *asked*, instead of being ordered, shouted at or even pushed. And then to know that she had the choice of answering yes or even no. She had to be careful here, and so she said, with that cunning that comes from being treated like nothing for too long, 'What will you give me in return?'

It started off with a piece of rewari saved from the recent marriage feast to which they had not invited her. She shared it promptly with Joseph, and from there it went on until, at the end of the week, she had for him a top without a point, three plastic bangles for herself, first place at the tap on two occasions when she overslept and was late, and even an invitation to a not-so-important doll's marriage.

For only the first week that was a good run of luck indeed, and Lata had reason to feel happy. The conditions laid down for the wearing of her shoe were stern. It must never touch the ground, nor be scuffed against anything to wear away the gold. This was no ordinary shoe, and therefore it must be treated as no ordinary shoe was ever treated. Such conditions were bound to affect the wearer too. The betel seller's daughter borrowed the shoe for a whole afternoon, and she wore it when her relatives called on the family from their village. All through the visit she sat sedately on a trunk, one leg folded under her and the other hanging down.

'What a beautiful pair of shoes!' cried her girl cousins, green with envy.

'What a modest well-behaved girl!' said the elders—which she certainly was not. But for this excellent piece of foolery, the shoe earned Lata twenty-five paise, with which she and Joseph treated themselves to gaudy pink balls of ice on sticks. They never bought these things because, as they argued— after they were eaten—they were nothing but frozen water after all, weren't they? And they had to be eaten fast; otherwise they melted down one's chin and were wasted. However, now Lata and Joseph could allow themselves such extravagance because the shoe held out promise of more to come.

'If we sold it, we could easily get a thousand rupees!' cried Joseph, his eyes shining.

Perhaps that was wishful thinking—but being raja no longer was, and it was a proud moment when Lata was allowed to climb to the coveted position between Janak Seth's broad feet, wearing the shoe and holding the stick aloft to start the game. Shabby she was, and shabby she would remain—but at last she had something about which she could feel important. And this the shoe had done for her.

Unfortunately, even the most enchanted of shoes have a way of growing too small for one's feet, and there came a time when Lata couldn't wear her gold and red shoe any more. The felt inner sole had become dirty from all the grubby feet that had worn it, the gold thread was not so gold any more, and the whole shoe had begun to show wear and even a little tear in its velvet. But even if Lata and every other child in the lane outgrew it, there was still one person not likely to do so. With a little wad of paper stuffed into its toe, the shoe would always fit Joseph. That was the way he wore it the first time Lata lifted him into place between Janak Seth's broad feet. Sitting under the gentle curve of Seth's large round stomach, he seemed smaller than ever, but he was smiling.

He looked down at all the faces turned up to him. To think that he, poor little Joseph Pinto the Legless One, had the power in this hand that held the rod to make all those children stop or go just as *he* chose! The thought almost brought tears to his eyes.

'Joseph is raja!' cried Lata, clapping her hands. 'Joseph is raja for forever!'

'Janak Raja went to Dilli...' the children chanted.

So Joseph too became a raja, and because of his shrivelled legs, it was possible he might be raja forever. This was far better than pretending to believe he could ever become a jet-plane pilot, an engine driver or even an egret.

Illustrated by Tapas Guha

Pankaj Bisht

•

FROM **BHOLU AND GOLU**

This is the story of a small bear, Bholu, who is captured and trained to perform in a circus. He is forced to dance, play football with the clowns, sometimes pretend to wrestle. For every small mistake he is whipped by the ringmaster. The only thing Bholu enjoys is riding a motorcycle. He misses his parents and his home in the jungle, and longs to return to them.

Golu, the son of a mahout, befriends the bear and decides to help him escape from the circus.

Sleep didn't come easily to Golu that night. When he finally dozed off, he was still thinking about how he could help Bholu.

He dreamt he was riding pillion on a motorcycle—a beautiful red motorcycle. The motorcycle belonged to the ringmaster, and Bholu was riding it in the dream. It was moving at top speed and he was enjoying himself. The wind whistled past, ruffling his hair and tousling Bholu's. He held the bear tightly. Bholu was singing joyfully:

The motorcycle,
It's quite a thing.
Go up a mountain
Or down a hill.

Give it a kick
And it will start.
Run with the wind
And don't lose heart.

Those who scold you,
Hit you, whip you,
Those who butt you,
Beat you, bash you,

Those who slug you,
Club you, stun you,
Those who thrash you,
Cane you, strike you,

The brutal and the rough,
The cruel and the unkind,
You'll leave them all behind.

'Come back, come back!'
The ringmaster pleads
With folded hands and bended knees.

'I'll treat you well
This time,' he'll say,
Don't listen to him,
Just ride away.

Golu sang with Bholu. The motorcycle sped along, racing with the wind. They were headed for Bholu's home. The mountain road wound through the forest. The bear's home was nearby. They were almost there when somebody called Golu, and he woke up. It was his father. 'How much longer will you stay in bed, Golu? Look, it's morning.'

After breakfast, just as his father was leaving, Golu said, 'Can I ask you something, Bapu?'

'Yes, go ahead,' said his father, patting him affectionately.

'Bapu, why are the animals so afraid of the ringmasters?'

'Because of the whip,' his father replied, smiling.

'But animals are stronger than human beings, aren't they, Bapu? What if they snatched away the whip?'

Bapu laughed. 'Son, a strong body is not everything. Human beings also have brains and can think. Have you ever asked yourself why only man can use the whip or goad? Why can't the elephant or the lion? Or for that matter, your friend the bear?'

'Because animals are good. They don't beat people and force them to dance. They don't ride on others' backs, either. They use their own feet.'

Bapu laughed again and said, 'Well, you're right, son. But animals aren't as intelligent as men. Even if an animal were to snatch the whip, what would he do with it? We have many ways to trap and hold animals.'

'How?'

'Well, we've got nets and cages. If an animal gets out of control, we even have guns. They can be shot. Haven't you seen that during circus shows there is a man standing by with a gun? The gun isn't there just for show!'

'And now can I go?' asked Bapu. 'It's getting late. The elephants must be hungry and anxious. They should be fed.'

'Just one more question, Bapu,' said Golu.

'Your questions are unending. I've got work to do.'

'Just one more!' pleaded Golu. 'Why do humans capture animals?'

'Since when have you become king of the jungle?' joked Bapu.

'Tell me, Bapu!' Golu insisted.

'They capture animals to use them and for their own amusement, what else?' said Bapu and went off to work. Golu just sat there, thinking quietly. It was wrong of people to keep animals captive for selfish reasons.

Golu got up and went straight to the bear. 'Look, Bholu,' he said, 'if animals are scared of humans, that's only right. Men are wicked. They have guns. They don't hesitate to shoot animals. Don't try to snatch the whip. It could be very dangerous. I'll think of some other plan.'

They played football for a while. Suddenly Golu remembered the previous night's dream. He told Bholu about it. The bear was delighted.

After racking his brains, Golu even remembered a few lines of the song. He sang them aloud:

The motorcycle,
It's quite a thing.
Go up a mountain
Or down a hill.

Bholu loved the song. He swayed and danced to it for a long time. Golu laughed and sang the song again and again. Suddenly an idea struck Golu. 'Hey listen!' he shouted.

The bear stopped dancing and looked at him.

'You know how to ride a motorcycle, don't you?'

The bear nodded.

Bholu couldn't understand what the boy meant.

'Run away. Just like you did in the dream!'

Bholu liked the idea! He made little noises of approval.

'But the motorcycle you ride in the circus is no good. You need a new one, don't you agree? Like the one the ringmaster has,' said Golu.

At the mere mention of the ringmaster Bholu became agitated. He shook his head and went on shaking it—no, no, no.

'Don't worry,' Golu said, putting his arm around Bholu's shoulder reassuringly. 'It wouldn't be stealing. When you've covered some distance, you can abandon the motorcycle and walk. Do you understand?'

But the bear wasn't reassured. He was still frightened. He continued to shake his head. Golu could guess why the bear was scared. If he was caught trying to escape, the punishment the ringmaster would mete out to him would be terrible. He might even shoot him. Golu knew his plan could turn out to be dangerous. He thought about it all night. There were several problems. There was a chowkidar at the gate. It was not easy to get past him. He had a gun. Then, they needed a new motorcycle and only the ringmaster had one. It wouldn't be easy to get it from him. Besides, Golu had no idea where the bear's home was or how far it was. However, he realized that if the bear was to be free, they would have to take a few risks.

The next day Golu took a look at the circus boundary. It was made of tin sheets hammered onto wooden supports. At one place the tin sheets were loose. He tugged a little and the nails almost fell off. He quietly put them back. He knew it would be quite easy to remove the tin sheets and make an opening big enough to let through not only Bholu but the motorcycle as well.

Then he remembered that Bholu did not know how to start the motorcycle. During the show somebody started it before handing it over to Bholu. Only then was he able to ride it. And Golu hadn't a clue as to how to handle it himself. He'd only sat on one in his dream and that too with the bear driving. Nobody would let him ride the motorbike, he was certain. All he could do was to carefully observe how the ringmaster rode it.

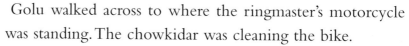

Golu walked across to where the ringmaster's motorcycle was standing. The chowkidar was cleaning the bike.

Golu asked, 'Chowkidar Uncle, what are you doing?'

'Sahib is going out. So I'm cleaning the bike for him.'

'When will he go?' Golu asked.

'I think he's just about to leave.'

'Uncle, do you know how to ride a bike?' Golu asked casually.

'I've never driven one, son, though I've seen others do so. First you insert a key, then give it a kick to get it started,' said the watchman and gave the motorcycle a kick to demonstrate.

'But why didn't it start?' asked Golu.

'I told you that a key has to be inserted. It won't start without it.'

'Where do you insert the key?' asked Golu again.

The watchman showed him where the key was inserted.

'And where is the key?' Golu asked.

'It's with Sahib. Have you been to his tent? It hangs from a nail on the middle pole.'

'Uncle, can I try and start it?' asked the boy.

'Sahib will be here any minute. He'll be angry. Besides, you're still a child. When you're grown-up you can get a motorcycle for yourself and ride it. But not this one. It's too big. If it fell on you, you'd get hurt.'

'I'll only give it one kick,' Golu said. 'Just once, please!'

'No. If Sahib comes he'll scold both of us.'

'Just once!' the boy pleaded again.

'Look, don't be obstinate,' said the chowkidar, trying to reason with the boy. Dejected, Golu gazed silently at the bike.

Finally, the chowkidar took pity on him. 'Okay, give it a kick quickly.'

The chowkidar straightened the start lever. At first the boy could not kick hard enough, but after a while he succeeded.

The chowkidar's eyes were glued to the ringmaster's tent. Suddenly, he pushed Golu away from the motorcycle. The ringmaster was approaching. He had a red helmet in his hand. He put on the helmet, fitted the key, kicked the motorcycle sharply, and within seconds, was out of the circus grounds, lost in the crowd beyond.

Golu wandered about for a while, then sat down near the ringmaster's tent.

The ringmaster returned quite soon. He parked the motorcycle, took off the helmet, and swinging the key on a chain, went inside the tent. Peeping into the tent through a hole, Golu saw the ringmaster put the helmet on a table and hang the key on the pole.

Golu ran to Bholu and told him his plan. Bholu was dumbfounded. Golu explained, 'Look, you must rise to the occasion. Don't be scared. Just do what I tell you, and don't worry.'

Excerpt from the chapter 'Golu's Dream'
Text translated by Sara Rai, verses by Arvind Krishna Mehrotra

Illustrated by Bindia Thapar

•

SNAKE TROUBLE

After retiring from the Indian Railways and settling in Dehra, Grandfather often enlivened his days (and ours) by keeping unusual pets. He paid a snake-charmer in the bazaar twenty rupees for a young python. Then, to the delight of a curious group of boys and girls, he slung the python over his shoulder and brought it home.

I was with Grandfather at the time and felt very proud walking beside him. He was popular in Dehra, especially among the more humble people, and everyone greeted him respectfully without seeming to notice the python. They were, in fact, quite used to seeing him in the company of strange creatures.

The first to see us arrive was Toto the monkey, who was swinging from a branch of the jackfruit tree. One look at the python, ancient enemy of his race, and he fled into the house squealing with fright. Then our parrot, Popeye, who had his perch in the veranda, set up the most awful shrieking and whistling. His whistle was like that of a steam engine. He had learnt to do this in earlier days, when we had lived near railway stations.

The noise brought Grandmother to the veranda, where she nearly fainted at the sight of the python curled round Grandfather's neck.

Grandmother was tolerant of most of his pets, but she drew the line at reptiles. Even a sweet-tempered lizard made her blood run cold. There was little chance that she would allow a python in the house.

'It will strangle you to death!' she cried.

'Nonsense,' said Grandfather. 'He's only a young fellow.'

'He'll soon get used to us,' I added, by way of support.

'He might, indeed,' said Grandmother, 'but I have no intention of getting used to him. And your Aunt Ruby is coming to stay with us tomorrow. She'll leave the minute she knows there's a snake in the house.'

'Well, perhaps we should show it to her first thing,' said Grandfather, who found Aunt Ruby rather tiresome.

'Get rid of it right away,' said Grandmother.

'I can't let it loose in the garden. It might find its way into the chicken shed, and then where will we be!'

'Minus a few chickens,' I said reasonably, but this only made Grandmother more determined to banish the python.

'Lock that awful thing in the bathroom,' she said. 'Go and find the man you bought it from, give him twenty rupees or twice as much, and get him to come here and collect it! He can keep the money you gave him.'

Grandfather and I took the snake into the bathroom and placed it in an empty tub. Looking a bit crestfallen, he said, 'Perhaps your Grandmother is right. I'm not worried about Aunt Ruby, but we don't want the python to get hold of Toto or Popeye.'

We hurried off to the bazaar in search of the snake-charmer but hadn't gone far when we found several snake-charmers looking for us. They had heard that Grandfather was buying snakes, and they had brought with them snakes of various sizes and descriptions.

'No, no!' protested Grandfather. 'We don't want more snakes. We want to return the one we bought.'

But the man who had sold it to us had, apparently, returned to his village in the jungle, looking for another python for Grandfather; and the other snake-charmers were not interested in buying, only in selling. In order to shake them off, we had to return home by a roundabout route, climbing a wall and cutting through an orchard. We found Grandmother pacing up and down the veranda. One look at our faces and she knew we had failed in our mission.

'All right,' said Grandmother. 'Just take it away yourselves, and see that it doesn't come back.'

'We'll get rid of it, Granny,' I said confidently. 'Don't you worry.'

Grandfather opened the bathroom door and stepped into the room. I was close behind him. We couldn't see the python anywhere.

'He's gone,' announced Grandfather.

'We left the window open,' I said.

'Deliberately, no doubt,' said Grandmother. 'But it couldn't have gone far. You'll have to search the grounds.'

A careful search was made of the house, the roof, the kitchen, the garden and the chicken shed, but there was no sign of the python.

'He must have gone over the garden wall,' Grandfather said cheerfully. 'He'll be well away by now!'

The python did not reappear, and when Aunt Ruby arrived with enough luggage to indicate that she had come for a long visit, there was only the parrot to greet her with a series of long, ear-splitting whistles.

For a couple of days Grandfather and I were a little worried that the python might make a sudden reappearance, but when he didn't show up again we felt he had gone for good. Aunt Ruby had to put up with Toto the monkey making faces at her, something I did only when she wasn't looking; and she complained that Popeye shrieked loudest when she was in the room; but she was used to them, and knew she would have to put up with them if she was going to stay with us.

And then, one evening, we were startled by a scream from the garden.

Seconds later Aunt Ruby came flying up the veranda steps, gasping, 'In the guava tree. I was reaching for a guava when I saw it staring at me. The look in its eyes! As though it would eat me alive—'

'Calm down, dear,' urged Grandmother, sprinkling rose water over my aunt. 'Tell us, what did you see?'

'A snake!' sobbed Aunt Ruby. 'A great boa constrictor in the guava tree. Its eyes were terrible, and it looked at me in such a queer way.'

'Trying to tempt you with a guava, no doubt!' said Grandfather turning away to hide his smile. He gave me a meaningful look, and I hurried out into the garden. But when I got to the guava tree, the python (if it had been the python) had gone.

'Aunt Ruby must have frightened it off,' I told Grandfather.

'I'm not surprised,' he said. 'But it will be back. I think it's taken a fancy to your aunt.'

Sure enough, the python began to make brief but frequent appearances, usually turning up in the most unexpected places.

One morning I found him curled up on a dressing-table, gazing at his own reflection in the mirror. I went for Grandfather, but by the time we returned the python had moved on.

He was seen again in the garden, and one day I spotted him climbing the iron ladder to the roof. I set off after him, and was soon up the ladder, which I had ascended many times. I stood up on the flat roof just in time to see the snake disappearing down a drainpipe. The end of his tail was visible for a few moments and then that too disappeared.

'I think he lives in the drainpipe,' I told Grandfather.

'Where does he get his food?' asked Grandmother.

'Probably lives on those field rats that used to be such a nuisance. Remember, they used to live in the drainpipe too.'

'Hmm...' Grandmother looked thoughtful. 'A snake has its uses. Well, as long as he keeps to the roof and prefers rats to chickens...'

But the python did not confine himself to the roof. Piercing shrieks from Aunt Ruby had us all rushing to her room. There was the python on her dressing-table, apparently admiring himself in the mirror.

'All the attention he's been getting has probably made him conceited,' said Grandfather picking up the python to the accompaniment of further shrieks from Aunt Ruby. 'Would you like to hold him for a minute, Ruby? He seems to have taken a fancy to you.'

Aunt Ruby ran from the room and on to the veranda, where she was greeted with whistles of derision from Popeye the parrot. Poor Aunt Ruby, she cut short her stay by a week and returned to Lucknow, where she was a schoolteacher. She said she felt safer in her school than she did in our house.

Having seen Grandfather handle the python with such ease and confidence, I decided I would do likewise. So the next time I saw the snake climbing the ladder to the roof, I climbed up alongside him. He stopped in his ascent, and I stopped too. I put out my hand, and he slid over my arm and up to my shoulder. As I did not want him coiling round my neck, I gripped him with both hands and carried him down to the garden. He didn't seem to mind.

The snake felt rather cold and slippery and at first he gave me goose pimples. But I soon got used to him, and he must have liked the way I handled him, because when I set him down he wanted to climb up my leg. As I had other things to do, I dropped him in a large, empty basket that had been left out in the garden. He stared out at me with unblinking, expressionless eyes. There was no way of knowing what he was thinking, if indeed he thought at all.

Just when all of us, including Grandmother, were getting used to having the python about the house and grounds, it was decided that we would be going to Lucknow for a few months.

Aunt Ruby lived and worked there. We would be staying with her, and so of course we couldn't take any pythons, monkeys or other unusual pets with us.

'What about Popeye?' I asked.

'Popeye isn't a pet,' said Grandmother. 'He's one of us. He comes too.'

And so the Dehra railway platform was thrown into confusion by the shrieks and whistles of our parrot, who could imitate both the guard's whistle and the whistle of a train. People dashed into their compartments, thinking the train was about to leave, only to realize that the guard hadn't blown his whistle after all. When they got down, Popeye would let out another shrill whistle, which sent everyone rushing for the train again. This happened several times until the guard actually blew his whistle. Nobody bothered to get on, and several passengers were left behind.

'Can't you gag that parrot?' asked Grandfather, as the train moved out of the station and picked up speed.

'I'll do nothing of the sort,' said Grandmother. 'I've bought a ticket for him, and he's entitled to enjoy the journey as much as anyone.'

It was to be a night journey, and presently Grandmother covered herself with a blanket and stretched herself out on the berth. 'It's been a tiring day. I think I'll go to sleep,' she said.

'Aren't we going to eat anything?' I asked.

'I'm not hungry—I had something before we left the house. You two help yourselves from the picnic hamper.'

Grandmother dozed off, and even Popeye started nodding, lulled to sleep by the clackety-clack of the wheels and the steady puffing of the steam engine.

'Well, I'm hungry,' I said. 'What did Granny make for us?'

'Stuffed parathas, omelettes and a tandoori chicken. It's all in the hamper under the berth.'

I tugged at the cane box and dragged it into the middle of the compartment. The straps were loosely tied. No sooner had I undone them than the lid flew open, and I let out a gasp of surprise.

In the hamper was our python, curled up contentedly. There was no sign of our dinner.

'It's the python,' I said. 'And it's finished all our dinner.'

'Nonsense,' said Grandfather, joining me near the hamper. 'Pythons won't eat omelettes and parathas. They like their food alive! Why, this is an old hamper, which was stored in the box room. The one with our food in it must have been left behind!'

Grandfather snapped the hamper shut and pushed it back beneath the berth.

'Don't let Grandmother see him,' he said. 'She might think we brought him along on purpose.'

'Well, I'm hungry,' I complained.

'Wait till we get to the next station, then we can buy some pakoras. Meanwhile, try some of Popeye's green chillies.'

'No thanks,' I said. 'You have them, Grandad.'

And Grandfather, who could eat chillies plain, popped a couple into his mouth and munched away contentedly.

A little after midnight there was a great clamour at the end of the corridor. Popeye made complaining squawks, and Grandfather and I got up to see what was wrong.

Suddenly there were cries of 'Snake, snake!'

I looked under the berth. The hamper was open.

'The python's out,' I said, and Grandfather dashed out of the compartment in his pyjamas. I was close behind.

About a dozen passengers were bunched together outside the washroom door.

'Anything wrong?' asked Grandfather casually.

'We can't get into the toilet,' said someone. 'There's a huge snake inside.'

'Let me take a look,' said Grandfather. 'I know all about snakes.'

The passengers made way and Grandfather and I entered the washroom together, but there was no sign of the python.

'He must have got out through the ventilator,' said Grandfather. 'By now he'll be in another compartment!' Emerging from the washroom, he told the assembled passengers, 'It's gone! Nothing to worry about. Just a harmless young python.'

When we got back to our compartment, Grandmother was sitting up on her berth.

'I knew you'd do something foolish behind my back,' she scolded. 'You told me you'd left that creature behind, and all the time it was with us on the train.'

Grandfather tried to explain that we had nothing to do with it, that the python had smuggled itself into the hamper, but Grandmother was unconvinced.

'Anyway, it's gone,' said Grandfather. 'It must have fallen out of the washroom window. We're over a hundred miles from Dehra, so you'll never see it again.'

Even as he spoke, the train slowed down and lurched to a grinding halt.

'No station here,' said Grandfather, putting his head out of the window.

Someone came rushing along the embankment, waving his arms and shouting.

'I do believe it's the stoker,' said Grandfather. 'I'd better go and see what's wrong.'

'I'm coming too,' I said, and together we hurried along the length of the stationary train until we reached the engine.

'What's up?' called Grandfather. 'Anything I can do to help? I know all about engines.'

But the engine-driver was speechless. And who could blame him? The python had curled itself about his legs, and the driver was too petrified to move.

'Just leave it to us,' said Grandfather, and dragging the python off the driver, he dumped the snake in my arms. The engine-driver sank down on the floor, pale and trembling.

'I think I'd better drive the engine,' said Grandfather, 'we don't want to be late getting into Lucknow. Your aunt will be expecting us!' And before the astonished driver could protest, Grandfather had released the brakes and set the engine in motion.

'We've left the stoker behind,' I said.

'Never mind. You can shovel the coal.'

Only too glad to help Grandfather drive an engine, I dropped the python in the driver's lap, and started shovelling coal. The engine picked up speed and we were soon rushing through the darkness, sparks flying skywards and the steam whistle shrieking almost without pause.

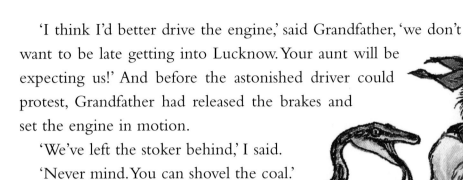

'You're going too fast!' cried the driver.

'Making up for lost time,' said Grandfather. 'Why did the stoker run away?'

'He went for the guard. You've left them both behind!'

Early next morning the train steamed safely into Lucknow. Explanations were in order, but as the Lucknow stationmaster was an old friend of Grandfather's all was well. We had arrived twenty minutes early, and while Grandfather went off to have a cup of tea with the engine-driver and the stationmaster, I returned the python to the hamper and helped Grandmother with the luggage. Popeye stayed perched on Grandmother's shoulder, eyeing the busy platform with deep distrust. He was the first to see Aunt Ruby striding down the platform, and let out a warning whistle.

Aunt Ruby, a lover of good food, immediately spotted the picnic hamper, picked it up and said, 'It's quite heavy. You must have kept something for me! I'll carry it out to the taxi.'

'We hardly ate anything,' I said.

'It seems ages since I tasted something cooked by your Granny.' And after that there was no getting the hamper away from Aunt Ruby.

Glancing at it, I thought I saw the lid bulging, but I had tied it down quite firmly this time and there was little likelihood of its suddenly bursting open.

Grandfather joined us outside the station and we were soon settled inside the taxi. Aunt Ruby gave instructions to the driver and we shot off in a cloud of dust.

'I'm dying to see what's in the hamper,' said Aunt Ruby. 'Can't I take just a little peek?'

'Not now,' said Grandfather, 'first let's enjoy the breakfast you've got waiting for us.'

Popeye, perched proudly on Grandmother's shoulder, kept one suspicious eye on the quivering hamper.

When we got to Aunt Ruby's house, we found breakfast laid out on the dining-table.

'It isn't much,' said Aunt Ruby. 'But we'll supplement it with what you've brought in the hamper.'

Placing the hamper on the table, she lifted the lid and peered inside...and promptly fainted.

Grandfather picked up the python, took it into the garden and draped it over a branch of a pomegranate tree.

When Aunt Ruby recovered, she insisted that she had seen a huge snake in the picnic hamper. We showed her the empty basket.

'You're seeing things,' said Grandfather. 'You've been working too hard.'

'Teaching is a taxing profession,' I said solemnly.

Grandmother said nothing. But Popeye broke into loud squawks and whistles, and soon everyone, including a slightly hysterical Aunt Ruby, was doubled up with laughter.

Illustrated by Atanu Roy

Anita Desai

·

GAMES AT TWILIGHT

It was still too hot to play outdoors. They had had their tea, they had been washed and had their hair brushed, and after the long day of confinement in the house that was not cool but at least a protection from the sun, the children strained to get out. Their faces were red and bloated with the effort, but their mother would not open the door; everything was still curtained and shuttered in a way that stifled the children, made them feel that their lungs were stuffed with cotton wool and their noses with dust and if they didn't burst out into the light and see the sun and feel the air, they would choke.

'Please, Ma, please,' they begged. 'We'll play in the veranda and porch, we won't go a step out of the porch.'

'You will, I know you will, and then—'

'No, we won't, we won't,' they wailed so horrendously that she actually let down the bolt of the front door so that they burst out like seeds from a crackling, overripe pod into the veranda, with such wild, maniacal yells that she retreated to her bath and the shower of talcum powder and the fresh sari that were to help her face the summer evening.

They faced the afternoon. It was too hot. Too bright. The white walls of the veranda glared stridently in the sun. The bougainvillea hung about it, purple and magenta, in livid balloons. The garden outside was like a tray made of beaten brass, flattened out on the red gravel and the stony soil in all shades of metal—aluminium, tin, copper and brass. No life stirred at this arid time of day—the birds still drooped, like dead fruit, in the papery tents of the tree;

some squirrels lay limp on the wet earth under the garden tap. The outdoor-dog lay stretched as if dead on the veranda mat, his paws and ears and tail all reaching out like dying travellers in search of water. He rolled his eyes at the children—two white marbles rolling in the purple sockets, begging for sympathy—and attempted to lift his tail in a wag but could not. It only twitched and lay still.

Then, perhaps roused by the shrieks of the children, a band of parrots suddenly fell out of the eucalyptus tree, tumbled frantically in the still, sizzling air, then sorted themselves out into battle formation and streaked away across the white sky.

The children, too, felt released. They began tumbling, shoving, pushing against each other, frantic to start. Start what? Start their business. The business of the children's day which is play.

'Let's play hide-and-seek.'

'Who'll be *It*?'

'You be *It*.'

'Why should I? You be.'

'You're the eldest.'

'That doesn't mean—'

The shoves became harder. Some kicked out. The motherly Mira intervened. She pulled the boys roughly apart. There was a tearing sound of cloth but it was lost in the heavy panting and angry grumbling and no one paid attention to the small sleeve hanging loosely off a shoulder.

'Make a circle, make a circle!' she shouted, firmly pulling and pushing till a kind of vague circle was formed. 'Now clap!' she roared and, clapping, they all chanted in melancholy unison: 'Dip, dip, dip—my blue ship,' and every now and then one or the other saw he was safe by the way his hands fell at the crucial moment—palm, or back of hand on palm—and dropped out of the circle with a yell and a jump of relief and jubilation.

Raghu was *It*. He started to protest, to cry, 'You cheated—Mira cheated—

Anu cheated—' but it was too late, the others had all already streaked away. There was no one to hear when he called out, 'Only in the veranda—the porch—Ma said—Ma said to stay in the porch!' No one had stopped to listen, all he saw were their brown legs flashing through the dusty shrubs, scrambling up brick walls, leaping over compost heaps and hedges, and then the porch stood empty in the purple shade of the bougainvillea and the garden was as empty as before; even the limp squirrels had whisked away, leaving everything gleaming, brassy and bare.

Only small Manu suddenly reappeared, as if he had dropped out of an invisible cloud or from a bird's claw, and stood for a moment in the centre of the yellow lawn, chewing his finger and near to tears as he heard Raghu shouting, with his head pressed against the veranda wall, 'Eighty-three, eighty-five, eighty-nine, ninety...' and then made off in a panic, half of him wanting to fly north, the other half counselling south. Raghu turned just in time to see the flash of his white shorts and the uncertain skittering of his red sandals, and charged after him with such a blood-curdling yell that Manu stumbled over the hosepipe, fell into its rubber coils and lay there weeping, 'I won't be *It*—you have to find them all—all—All!'

'I know I have to, idiot,' Raghu said, superciliously kicking him with his toe. 'You're dead,' he said with satisfaction, licking the beads of perspiration off his upper lip, and then stalked off in search of worthier prey, whistling spiritedly so that the hiders should hear and tremble.

Ravi heard the whistling

and picked his nose in a panic, trying to find comfort by burrowing the finger deep-deep into that soft tunnel. He felt himself too exposed, sitting on an upturned flowerpot behind the garage. Where could he burrow? He could run around the garage if he heard Raghu come—around and around and around—but he hadn't much faith in his short legs when matched against Raghu's long, hefty, hairy footballer legs. Ravi had a frightening glimpse of them as Raghu combed the hedge of crotons and hibiscus, trampling delicate ferns underfoot as he did so. Ravi looked about him desperately, swallowing a small ball of snot in his fear.

The garage was locked with a great heavy lock to which the driver had the key in his room, hanging from a nail on the wall under his work-shirt. Ravi had peeped in and seen him still sprawling on his string cot in his vest and striped underpants, the hair on his chest and the hair in his nose shaking with the vibrations of his phlegm-obstructed snores. Ravi had wished he were tall enough, big enough to reach the key on the nail, but it was impossible, beyond his reach for years to come. He had sidled away and sat dejectedly on the flowerpot. That at least was cut to his own size.

But next to the garage was another shed with a big green door. Also locked. No one even knew who had the key to the lock. That shed wasn't opened more than once a year when Ma turned out all the old broken bits of furniture and rolls of matting and leaking buckets, and the white anthills were broken and swept away and Flit sprayed into the spider webs and rat holes so that the whole operation was like the looting of a poor, ruined and conquered city. The green leaves of the door sagged. They were nearly off their rusty hinges. The hinges were large and made a small gap between the door and the walls only just large enough for rats, dogs and, possibly, Ravi to slip through.

Ravi had never cared to enter such a dark and depressing mortuary of defunct household goods seething with such unspeakable and alarming animal life but, as Raghu's whistling grew angrier and sharper and his crashing and storming in the hedge wilder, Ravi suddenly slipped off the flowerpot and through the crack and was gone. He chuckled aloud with astonishment at his own temerity so that Raghu came out of the hedge, stood silent with his hands on his hips, listening, and finally shouted, 'I heard you! I'm coming! *Got you*,' and came charging round the garage only to find the upturned flowerpot, the yellow dust, the crawling of white ants in a mud-hill against the closed shed door—nothing. Snarling he bent to pick up a stick and went off, whacking it against the garage and shed walls as if to beat out his prey.

Ravi shook, then shivered with delight, with self-congratulation. Also with fear. It was dark, spooky in the shed. It had a muffled smell, as of graves. Ravi had once got locked into the linen cupboard and sat there weeping for half an hour before he was rescued. But at least that had been a familiar place, and even smelt pleasantly of starch, laundry and, reassuringly, of his mother. But the shed smelt of rats, anthills, dust and spider webs. Also of less definable, less recognizable horrors. And it was dark. Except for the white-hot cracks along the door, there was no light. The roof was very low. Although Ravi was small, he felt as if he could reach up and touch it with his fingertips. But he didn't stretch. He hunched himself into a ball so as not to bump into anything, touch or feel anything. What might there not be to touch him and feel him as he stood there, trying to see in the dark? Something cold, or slimy—like a snake. Snakes! He leapt up as Raghu whacked the wall with his stick—then, quickly realizing what it was, felt almost relieved to hear Raghu, hear his stick. It made him feel protected.

But Raghu soon moved away. There wasn't a sound once his footsteps had gone around the garage and disappeared. Ravi stood frozen inside the shed. Then he shivered all over. Something had tickled the back of his neck. It took him a while to pick up the courage to lift his hand and explore. It was an insect—perhaps a spider—exploring him. He squashed it and wondered how many more creatures were watching him, waiting to reach out and touch him, the stranger.

There was nothing now. After standing in that position—his hand still on his neck, feeling the wet splodge of the squashed spider gradually dry—for minutes, hours, his legs began to tremble with the effort, the inaction. By now he could see enough in the dark to make out the large solid shapes of old wardrobes, broken buckets and bedsteads piled on top of each other around him. He recognized an old bathtub—patches of enamel glimmered at him and at last he lowered himself onto its edge.

He contemplated slipping out of the shed and into the fray. He wondered if it would not be better to be captured by Raghu and be returned to the milling crowd as long as he could be in the sun, the light, the free spaces of the garden and the familiarity of his brothers, sisters and cousins. It would be evening soon. Their games would become legitimate. The parents would sit out on the lawn on cane basket chairs and watch them as they tore around the garden or gathered in knots to share a loot of mulberries or black teeth-splitting jamun from the garden trees. The gardener would fix the hosepipe to the water tap and water would fall lavishly through the air to the ground, soaking the dry yellow grass and the red gravel and arousing the sweet, the intoxicating scent of water on dry earth—that loveliest scent in the world. Ravi sniffed for a whiff of it. He half-rose from the bathtub, then heard the despairing scream of one of the girls as Raghu bore down upon her. There was the sound of a crash, and of rolling about in the bushes, the shrubs, then screams and accusing sobs of, 'I touched the den—' 'You did not—' 'I did'— 'You liar, you did *not*' and then a fading away and silence again. Ravi sat back on the harsh edge of the tub, deciding to hold out a bit longer. What fun if they were all found and caught and he alone left unconquered! He had never known that sensation. Nothing more wonderful had ever happened to him than being taken out by an uncle and bought a whole slab of chocolate all to himself, or being flung into the soda-man's pony cart and driven up to the gate by the friendly driver with the red beard and pointed ears. To defeat Raghu, that hirsute, hoarse-voiced football champion would be thrilling beyond imagination. He hugged his knees together and smiled to himself almost shyly at the thought of so much victory, such laurels.

There he sat smiling, knocking his heels against the bathtub, now and then getting up and going to the door to put his ear to the broad crack and listening for sounds of the game, the pursuer and the pursued, and then returning to his seat with the dogged determination of the true winner, a breaker of records, a champion.

It grew darker in the shed as the light at the door grew softer, fuzzier, turned to a kind of crumbling yellow pollen that turned to yellow fur, blue fur, grey fur. Evening. Twilight. The sound of water gushing, falling. The scent of earth receiving water, slaking its thirst in great gulps and releasing that green scent of freshness, coolness. Through the crack Ravi saw the long purple shadows of the shed and the garage lying still across the yard. Beyond that, the white walls of the house. The bougainvillea had lost its lividity, hung in dark bundles that quaked and twittered and seethed with masses of humming sparrows. The lawn was shut off from his view. Could he hear the children's voices? It seemed to him that he could. It seemed to him that he could hear them chanting, singing, laughing. But what about the game? What had happened? Could it be over? How could it when he was still not found?

It then occurred to him that he could have slipped out long ago, dashed across the yard to the veranda and touched the 'den'. It was necessary to do that to win. He had forgotten. He had only remembered the part of hiding and trying to elude the seeker. He had done that so successfully, his success had occupied him so wholly that he had quite forgotten that success had to be clinched by that final dash to victory and the ringing cry of 'Den!'

With a whimper he burst through the crack, fell on his knees, got up and

stumbled on stiff, benumbed legs across the shadowy yard, crying heartily by the time he reached the veranda so that when he flung himself at the white pillar and bawled, 'Den! Den! Den!' his voice broke with rage and pity at the disgrace of it all and he felt himself flooded with tears and misery.

Out on the lawn, the children stopped chanting. They all turned to stare at him in amazement. Their faces were pale and triangular in the dusk. The trees and bushes around them stood inky and sepulchral, spilling long shadows across them. They stared, wondering at his reappearance, his passion, his wild animal howling. Their mother rose from her basket chair and came towards him, worried, annoyed, saying, 'Stop it, stop it, Ravi. Don't be a baby. Have you hurt yourself?' Seeing him attended to, the children went back to clasping their hands and chanting '*The grass is green, the rose is red...*'

But Ravi would not let them. He tore himself out of his mother's grasp and pounded across the lawn into their midst, charging at them with his head lowered so that they scattered in surprise. 'I won, I won, I won,' he bawled, shaking his head so that the big tears fled. 'Raghu didn't find me. I won, I won.'

It took them a minute to grasp what he was saying, even who he was. They had quite forgotten him. Raghu had found all the others long ago. There had been a fight about who was to be *It* next. It had been so fierce that their mother had emerged from her bath and made them change to another game. Then they had played another and another. Broken mulberries from the tree and eaten them. Helped the driver wash the car when their father returned from work. Helped the gardener water the beds till he roared at them and swore he would complain to their parents. The parents had come out, taken up their positions on the cane chairs. They had begun to play again, sing and chant. All this time no one had remembered Ravi. Having disappeared from the scene, he had disappeared from their minds. Clean.

'Don't be a fool,' Raghu said roughly, pushing him aside, and even Mira said, 'Stop howling, Ravi. If you want to play, you can stand at the end of the line,' and she put him there very firmly.

The game proceeded. Two pairs of arms reached up and met in an arc. The children trooped under it again and again in a lugubrious circle, ducking their heads and intoning:

The grass is green,
The rose is red;
Remember me
When I am dead, dead, dead, dead...

And the arc of thin arms trembled in the twilight, and the heads were bowed so sadly, and their feet tramped to that melancholy refrain so mournfully, so helplessly, that Ravi could not bear it. He would not follow them, he would not be included in this funeral game. He had wanted victory and triumph—not a funeral. But he had been forgotten, left out, and he would not join them now. The ignominy of being forgotten—how could he face it? He felt his heart go heavy and ache inside him unbearably. He lay down full length on the damp grass, crushing his face into it, no longer crying, silenced by a terrible sense of his insignificance.

Illustrated by Suddhasattwa Basu

Shashi Deshpande

·

FROM **THE NARAYANPUR INCIDENT**

The year is 1942—the time of the Quit India Movement. A teacher in a small town, a follower of Gandhiji, has been arrested. His elder son, eighteen-year-old Mohan, and his college friends, including Suman, believe in a more aggressive form of resistance to the British. His younger son, Babu, aged thirteen and daughter Manju, two years younger, are also keen to participate in the struggle against the British.

Manju woke up to the usual early morning sounds—the swishing sounds of someone washing a doorstep, the gurgling sounds of someone gargling, the chirp chirp of birds and the whirr whirr of Appa's charkha. Manju listened idly to these sounds, feeling, as she always did when she heard them, that everything was all right. And then, suddenly, she remembered that Appa had been arrested the day before. He was not at home and it would be a long time before she woke up to the sound of Appa spinning. But then, if it wasn't Appa, who could it be?

Frightened, Manju rushed out of the room. It was Amma spinning, sitting under the window to get the early morning light.

'Amma?' Manju asked in astonishment. 'Why are you spinning today?'

Amma could never spin regularly like Appa did. Sometimes, when she was in the mood, she would sit at the charkha for hours. Or else, she forgot about it for days together. Now Amma gave Manju a wan smile. 'I thought I'd try Appa's way of beginning a day,' she said.

Mohan's head popped in through the door that led to the back passage. 'She wants to surprise Appa by spinning enough to make a shirt for him,' he

said solemnly, spoiling it the next instant by giving Manju a huge grin.

Amma, without stopping or looking up, retorted, 'No, this one is going to be for you.'

Mohan, unlike Amma or Appa, wore clothes made out of mill cloth. 'What has independence to do with wearing hand-spun clothes and all that rot?' he would ask Appa impatiently. 'First, let's drive out the British. That should have top priority. All other things come next.'

'This spinning programme is more important than you imagine, Mohan,' Appa would exclaim. 'Unless we can provide work for ourselves, what use is independence?'

'Okay, Amma,' Mohan said now, 'it's a deal. You spin enough for a shirt and I'll wear it.'

'Amma,' Babu complained later, 'are you trying to give Mohan his shirt all in one day?'

Amma laughed. She had been sitting there for more than two hours now. Meanwhile Manju, under Amma's directions, had brought in the milk, boiled it, and swept and cleaned the kitchen. Babu had had his bath and was waiting for breakfast, while Mohan, whistling softly between his teeth, cleaned his bike.

'I'll get up now. Ooooh, I'm stiff. Oh, my poor legs!'

'Don't forget my shirt, Amma,' Mohan's voice came from the back passage. 'You can't get off by moaning about your legs.'

'You'll get your shirt, young man. Now, children, give me one hour and I'll have your meal ready. I have to go out myself after that.'

While the food was cooking, Amma plaited Manju's hair into one long neat plait. Babu had joined Mohan in his bike cleaning and Manju could hear a continuous buzz of conversation from the two of them. Soon after lunch, Mohan went off to college and Amma, after clearing up, went out too. She said she would be back in an hour.

Manju had just settled down with a book when she was startled by Babu's urgent hiss, almost in her ear, 'Manju, I say, Manju!'

Manju looked up from her book with a start. 'Oh, Babu, what is it? How you startled me!'

'Listen, I'm going out. Want to come with me?'

'Where?'

'I'll tell you later. If you want to come, just say so and come quickly.'

'But Amma?'

'We'll lock the house and leave the keys with Ramabai. We'll be home before Amma, anyway. Are you coming? If not, I'm off.'

Manju jumped up in a flurry. 'I'm coming. Wait for me.'

Babu was waiting with the huge lock and key when Manju came out. He locked the door, gave the lock a tug to make sure it was locked, then thrust the key at Manju.

'Go and give that to Ramabai.'

Manju held back. 'I'm not going. You go and give it.'

Ramabai, their nearest neighbour, was a prying, inquisitive woman. She had to know everything. Her questions were endless and came so fast that Mohan had nicknamed her 'A question-a-minute-Ramabai'.

'Don't be silly. You're just wasting time. Hurry up, now.'

'I don't like to go to her. She keeps asking questions.'

'So what? Just shut her up.'

'Why don't *you* shut her up?' Manju asked suspiciously. 'Are you scared of her?'

'Me? Scared of her? Ha ha! You're the one who seems to be scared of a snoopy old woman. And then you want to take part in the movement. Girls!'

Manju glared at him, snatched the key and said, 'I'll be back in a second.'

'Time for one question, anyway,' Babu grinned.

'Please give this to Amma when she returns. Babu and I are going out but we'll be back soon,' Manju gabbled, all in one breath and turned away before Ramabai could utter a word. She thought she had got away when Ramabai yelled, 'Hey, Manju, where are you going? Only Babu and you? Does your mother know? Where has she gone? Where's Mohan?'

'Don't know. Back soon,' Manju called back over her shoulder and fled.

'Now,' she asked Babu impatiently, 'tell me where we're going.'

'To watch a procession. Walk fast. We may be late.'

'What procession? Whose procession? Where?'

'You sound just like Ramabai,' Babu said. 'Did she give you a quick lesson?'

'Oh, shut up about Ramabai. Tell me, Babu, what procession? Don't be so mean.' Manju struggled to keep up with Babu's longer strides.

'The college students are taking out a procession from their college to the Collector's office. Mohan told me we could watch. He says it's going to be peaceful.'

There were already some people lining the roads. Manju and Babu found a good spot, almost opposite the gate of the Collector's compound. They had to wait for some time. In a while, it began to rain. It had been drizzling off and on since the morning. But this was a heavy downpour—the usual monsoon rain, heavy and steady. People rushed for shelter. Manju and Babu sheltered themselves under a large tamarind tree.

'Look at me!' Manju exclaimed. Her hair was plastered to her head, her clothes clung to her, a large drop hung on the top of her nose. She giggled at herself, but Babu, after a guffaw, said guiltily, 'Why don't you go home and change?'

Manju refused.

Soon they heard the magical words, 'They're coming, they're coming'. The children, like the others, rushed out, heedless of the rain. Policemen now

appeared all along the road. Some of then walked in front of the students, some by their sides; but the students marched as if the police didn't exist. They walked in complete silence. There were no slogans, no shouts, just the shuffle of feet, the drip drip of rain and a low murmur from the watching crowd.

Babu and Manju looked eagerly for Mohan. Yes, there he was, dressed in white pyjamas and a cream-coloured shirt, with another boy, both holding aloft a picture of the Mahatma. Their arms must have ached holding it up that way for so long, but their faces were expressionless.

Now the leaders of the procession—Suman was one of them, they saw in excitement—had reached the barred gates. A police officer—he was the DSP, Mohan told them later—came up to them. There was some conversation between him and the students. The students seemed to be arguing. The rain had lessened now and the police officer took off his hat and ruffled his hair. Once he laughed, showing all his teeth, but the students remained serious. One of them handed him a piece of paper. He took it without glancing at it and nodded. The students turned their backs on him and one of them shouted

'Mahatma Gandhi ki jai.'

'Jai,' the others shouted back loudly. And then they briskly marched back the way they had come.

'Is that all?' Manju asked in disappointment.

'What else did you want? A dance? A drama?' Babu asked scornfully. Nevertheless, he understood her feeling and asked Mohan the same question when he returned home. 'Why did you go back so quietly? Were you scared of what the police would do?'

Mohan seemed immensely pleased with himself. 'Scared? Not by a long chalk! We had planned it this way. We knew they would stop us at the gates. We knew they expected us to protest and be violent. Oh yes, they wanted us to do that so that they could beat us up and haul us away to jail. But we are not prepared to go to jail—not as yet, anyway. Not until we've given them much more trouble. And so we decided we would give them no chance at all.'

'What was the point then?' Babu asked, while Manju listened earnestly, her chin cupped in her hands.

'It's like a declaration of war. We've told them now—this is war for us and you're the enemy. You don't start a war without first declaring your intentions, do you?'

'Unless you're Adolf Hitler,' Amma, who had been quietly listening to them, said with a small smile.

'Right. Which we're not. So, that's how it was.'

'And what was that paper you gave the policeman?'

'That was a notice we served on the Collector, as a representative of His Majesty's government, asking them to quit India or face the consequences.'

Suman and another boy turned up after they had finished their dinner that night. The boy staggered in with a large newspaper-covered parcel in his hands.

'Got it?' Mohan asked, his voice tense with excitement.

'Yes. Lot of trouble, though. Where shall I take it?'

'Here, let me help you. My room okay, Amma?'

'No, I think the puja room is better. A light there will look more normal.'

'Right as usual, Amma. The puja room, then.'

The boy went away after a whispered conversation with Suman. Then Suman, Amma and Mohan went into the small puja room. Babu and Manju stared curiously over their shoulders at the mysterious parcel which turned out to be a cyclostyling machine.

'Babu,' Mohan said as they settled down to work, 'sit out in the front room and keep watch. Give us a warning if anyone seems to be coming to our house. Manju, go to bed. Or else,' he went on, noticing her crestfallen face, 'you sit here in the hall and pass on Babu's warning to us.'

Babu sat outside, alert and attentive. He felt a thickening in his throat. It was beginning. And at last he was doing something. What a pity Gopya, Murali and the others would never know about it. Perhaps, some day... He checked himself and kept his eyes and mind on the road outside. It was deserted. In a little while, the nine o'clock siren went off. Babu thought for the first time that day of the war being fought all over the world. And suddenly, coming out of his reverie, he tensed. A man riding a bike got off and stopped right outside their gate. But it was only to light a cigarette, it seemed. Babu could see the match flaring, then the glow in front of the man's face. The small point of light moved as the man got on his bike and rode away. One more bike. Yes, this man was getting off. Maybe, he too—no, he was opening their gate. Babu flung himself inside. Manju turned a startled face to him.

'Someone's coming in.'

There was silence. From inside the puja room, three faces looked at him blankly, the dim light giving them a peculiar look. Shadows quivered and danced as the wick in the oil lamp flickered and fizzed. Then Amma got up and came out, followed by Mohan. Suman stayed inside and Mohan closed the door of the room.

'Manju, go to bed. Babu, you too.'

There was a knock at the door. Babu rushed to his room, unrolled his

bedroll and threw himself on it.

A knock again.

'Who's there?' Amma called out.

Knock knock.

'Mohan, go and see who it is.'

Manju, who had got into bed too, noticed that though Amma's voice was steady, her hands trembled.

Mohan came in saying, 'Amma, it's Patil, the Sub-Inspector.'

Amma held Manju's hand in a tight, hurtful clutch, though her voice was still cool and calm. 'What does he want?'

'He wants to talk to you.'

'To me?'

The hand relaxed. Manju drew her own hand back and rubbed it softly.

'I haven't come to trouble you,' a strange voice said. 'Your husband was my friend in school. I'm a friend.'

Amma got up quickly and went out. Manju waited a moment and followed her. There was Babu coming out of his room, making a show of having been woken out of a deep sleep, rubbing his eyes, yawning loudly and repeatedly, mumbling in a grumpy voice, 'Who is it? Who is it?' But nobody paid him any attention and soon Babu was taking in everything with the greatest curiosity.

The man—was he really a police officer? He didn't look like one in his dingy clothes—was saying to Amma, 'Yes, we were in school together. Oh, he was far above me. He was a scholar and I was one of the dunces. He always helped me, though. God knows how often I would have been caned but for him.'

'Please, Patil saheb,' Amma said, rather impatiently, 'tell me why you are here.'

'It's like this.' Suddenly the man was brisk and businesslike. His glance swept over all of them, taking them all in shrewdly. Certainly this man was no dunce. 'There's going to be a search in your house.'

'When?'

'Most probably tonight. I heard the Saheb talking. They were speaking of a cyclostyling machine. It seems you people are making copies of the Mahatma's speech. They say you have people hiding here as well.'

'Ha!' Mohan scoffed.

'But you have the cyclostyling machine?'

'No!' Mohan said instantly.

'Have you?' the man asked Amma.

'No,' Mohan repeated angrily. 'You're wasting your time spying on us.'

'Tell me.' The man ignored Mohan and spoke to Amma.

'Yes,' Amma replied simply and Mohan made an angry hissing sound.

'Where is it?'

'Amma, you've gone...'

'Inside.'

Manju's heart began beating wildly. Why was Amma giving them away?

'Give it to me. I'll get it out of the way. You can have it when it's safe.'

Mohan burst out again. 'Amma, what are you doing? How can you trust a policeman?'

The man touched Mohan on the shoulder. 'Mohan, you're still very young. There are many things you don't understand. I am a policeman, yes, but your father was and still is my friend. And this is my country as much as it is yours. Now, give it to me quickly. They may come any moment.'

Amma opened the door of the puja room and said, 'Suman!'

Suman emerged, wiping her face with her sari, looking anxiously at them.

'Come in.' Amma beckoned to the man. 'It's here.'

Suman stared at Amma and the man in bewilderment. Amma smiled at her and said, 'You've got to get away, Suman. Take away all that material. Mohan, will you...?'

Mohan stared at Amma, at Suman and finally at Patil, who stared steadily back at Mohan. And suddenly the two smiled at each other.

'Okay, Amma,' Mohan said and ducked into the puja room. He lugged the machine out and gave it to Patil.

'Do you have a largish bag with you?' the man asked.

'Manju...' Amma began, but Babu had already got it.

'That's fine, that's fine,' the man said.

And then they were gone—Patil, Mohan and Suman. The house seemed unbelievably quiet after the earlier intense activity.

'Let's go back to bed,' Amma suggested.

Mohan came back shortly. 'Suman?' Manju asked him anxiously.

'She's all right.'

'Go to bed, Manju,' Amma said.

Bed? With the police about to come? But nevertheless, she did drop off at some time. And came out of her sleep with a jerk to hear a loud knock at the door. It was repeated. Manju sat up in sudden fright. Amma patted her comfortingly.

'Who is it?' she asked loudly.

'Open the door,' a strange voice ordered.

'Mohan, see who it is,' Amma said.

It was like going through something all over again. But this time they knew for sure it wasn't a friend standing out there. No need for Mohan to announce, 'Amma, it's the police.'

Excerpt from chapter iv

Illustrated by Subir Roy

Shama Futehally

·

THE TUNNEL

Ankush was looking out of the train window at the bustling platform. He refused to look anywhere else. He was not going to talk to Mummy or Papa or anybody. And he was not going to cry, he was not. Mummy was on the seat next to him, trying to make him talk, just the way he tried to make her talk sometimes. It was as if they had changed places for once. And there was Papa saying, 'Do you want a bat, Anku? Or a water pistol?'

A toy seller appeared near the window and suddenly there were lots of colours around Ankush's face. Pink, green and blue toys were all bobbing away together on the toy seller's cart. Ankush looked away again.

'What about a cricket set?' said Papa anxiously. 'You can play with it after you get there. Look, Anku, it has a picture of Sachin on it!'

And it really did. There was a first-class picture of Sachin, right on top of the plastic cover. It was a huge set, the sort of thing that Mummy and Papa might give him on his birthday. Papa had never before bought such a big present on an ordinary day. (But today everything was different.) Ankush shook his head, but the toy seller quickly took down the set and fortunately Papa bought it. He placed it carefully on the seat, next to Ankush's water bottle, and patted it two or three times.

A bell clanged somewhere on the platform. Mummy sat up with a jerk and Papa stiffened. Everyone on the platform suddenly began to hurry.

Now Mummy was clasping him tight, and over his head she spoke to Hari Singh who was at the door of the carriage. 'Hari Singh, just make sure he doesn't want water or anything.'

'Certainly, Bibiji. He is like my own child, have no fear.'

'And...' Mummy's voice sounded more and more wobbly...'remember he's frightened of tunnels.'

'Shoo-oo-ooo!' There was a piercing whistle which went through their bones. Now Mummy and Papa were both looking at him as if they were waiting to be punished. How funny it was, this feeling of having changed places with them!

One after the other they both gave him a tight long hug. He wanted to turn his face away and show them how angry he was, but instead of turning away he found himself waving bravely, first to one, then to the other. Now the train began to move as it always did in the beginning—very, very slowly, as if it was hardly moving at all. At once a huge pillar hid them from sight and they were gone.

They were gone, and that was it. Now there was only Hari Singh. 'Baba,' he said, 'don't worry about anything. Soon Mummy's operation will be over and we will be back. Look out of the window now, how nice it is.'

Hari Singh stroked Ankush's head with his big rough hands. 'I'll be back in a few minutes,' he said, taking a bidi out of his pocket. Then he was gone too. Ankush was all alone in the huge empty carriage. He had never been so alone before. The large green seat was empty except for his small lunch-box. In one corner somebody had left a pile of luggage covered with an old black cloth. Nothing else. That about-to-cry feeling began, as if ants were crawling about inside his mouth.

He looked up to make the feeling go away. He saw that even the 'upstairs' was empty. When Mummy and Papa were there he loved to go up. Papa would swing him up. Then Mummy would stretch her legs out on the lower seat and read her magazine.

He would wait till Papa gave him a signal, and then he would lean over and punch her magazine right in the middle. She never failed to shriek in fright. Never.

And then that tunnel business. Of course he wasn't really frightened of tunnels. He wasn't a baby. But it was so nice to feel frightened, when a huge whistle blew and everything went dark, and you were in Mummy's lap all the time. Now...

Ankush bit his lip bravely, because Papa had told him that he, Papa, knew Ankush would be brave. Look out of the window and you'll forget everything, Papa had said. Ankush turned to the window which was half-open. He pushed against it with one shoulder, as he had seen Papa do. It rose a little and then—WHAM!—it thundered as it slid down and dropped on his hand.

Oh, the pain was terrible. Ankush couldn't stop himself from crying out. He turned his face to the wall and his shoulders shook. And just then—Shree-ee-ee-eek! A whistle blew, so loudly that it seemed to hit him. And there was a noise like thunder, and everything went black.

It seemed the darkness and noise went on for hours, and Ankush's sobs turned into screams of terror. Just when he couldn't stand it for a minute longer, the dark began to slowly lift. And then Ankush saw a kind of magic happening.

The luggage in the corner was moving. It had got up and was coming towards him. A hand came out from under the black cloth and pushed aside the top part. And behind that part of the black cloth Ankush saw: MUMMY! Mummy? Was it? Wasn't it? Had Mummy hidden in the train to give him a surprise? She loved giving him surprises. But no, this face seemed a little

different. It had paan-stained lips and big gold earrings. This face looked like Mummy because it *talked* like Mummy.

'Oh, my little child, my little bird. So frightened? But it was only a tunnel. Why didn't you come to me? To my lap?'

The hand came out again and undid the whole cloth, and from underneath came out a complete auntie, rather plump, wearing a salwar-kameez and a very long dupatta around her head. She looked like Mummy did when she put her sari over her head in the sun. The auntie picked him up and sat down. He was on her lap. It felt nice, burying his face into the soft silky material, even though it was all a little different. It felt like the times when Mummy went out and Maasi came to stay with him. And now the new auntie was looking into his face and laughing.

'Goodness! Don't you ever talk? Or has Mummy told you to keep quiet all the way to Calcutta?'

Ankush began to giggle.

'There, at least you can laugh! Don't be frightened, my little one. Your auntie is here. Now, how about something nice to eat?'

She opened a plastic box and held up some delicious-looking round things like gulab jamuns.

Ankush nodded his head vigorously. 'I also want those triangle things,' he said. Somehow he didn't feel at all shy.

'No, I don't think you should have those. They are made of meat and your parents may not like it. You can have as many of these others as you want. But first you must clean your hands.'

And Ankush knew exactly what she was going to do. She was going to take out a little towel and pour some water on it (only she poured it from a glass bottle and Mummy from a thermos), then she would wipe his face and hands. The auntie spread a napkin on his lap and gave him a little thali full of the round things. They were very, very good.

While eating, Ankush looked at the auntie, a little shy. 'I thought you were

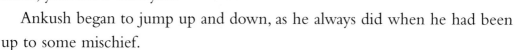

'luggage,' he said.

'What!'

'Because you were covered with that cloth.'

And then the auntie began to shake with laughter. She laughed till the tears ran down her cheeks and finally she gave him a pretend-slap. 'You little rascal, you! How dare you!'

Ankush began to jump up and down, as he always did when he had been up to some mischief.

'You are luggage, you are luggage! That's what you are!'

'No, I am not. I am your Saeeda auntie. That's what I am.'

'Luggage!' shouted Ankush, leaping into her lap.

Ankush tugged at her black covering. 'That's what you cover luggage with.'

'Maybe. But it's also what I cover myself with. And it's called a burqa.'

Just then Hari Singh came hurrying into the compartment. He looked at the two of them, a little puzzled, and then he said, 'Baba! I almost forgot. Were you frightened when we went through the tunnel?'

Sitting up in Saeeda auntie's lap, Ankush looked Hari Singh straight in the eye.

'Frightened? Who, me? OF COURSE NOT!' he said.

Illustrated by K.P. Sudesh

Mala Marwah

•

BIDESIA BABU

In Pipli town in Hazaribagh District of Bihar, lived Bidesia Babu. You might want to know why he was called Bidesia, or Videshia, or Foreigner Babu. It wasn't because he had travelled to distant lands or anything like that. About twenty years ago he had gone to visit his grandfather in village Kirimiri, and stayed away for two whole months. But because he had gone far away in a train, and come back wearing shiny new brown boots with black laces and a sola topee on his head, people thought he was a very well-travelled sort of man, so they called him Bidesia Babu. His real name was Debnath Chowdhury, but no one called him that, not even his own mother, who was nearly 100 years old.

Actually Bidesia Babu was two people. On weekdays he worked as a geologist in the Govt. Survey Office, and on Sundays he worked as an amateur INVENTOR and HOMEOPATHIC DOCTOR. Once the Raja of Hathi paid him a visit to present him with a mosquito-net embroidered with—can you believe it!—giant anopheles mosquitoes! For curing him of jungle malaria and hiccoughs; and the Chief Engineer developed a crick in his back (which Bidesia Babu then had to cure) when he bent to thank B.B. for filling the old coal quarry with water and turning it into a lake. Among the automatic can-openers and five-second math-problem-solvers that B. Babu invented, was his most famous invention. This was the Immediate Upstart Finder, a little box with big antennae that picked up nervous responses typical to troublemakers. As you may imagine, this was a terrific thing to have at a

mela, it always pointed out exactly who was going to plant a cracker under the Head Hawaldar's seat, or who was planning to purloin the payesh handi when the principal pujari was having forty winks.

Sometimes Bidesia Babu was heard singing:

Myself Bidesia
Babu am
Doing crazy things
yes-ji
If problem develop
I glad to hellop
Happy Inventoring-ji!

Well WHAT do you think happened one very quiet Sunday morning. The Immediate Upstart Finder antennae began waggling furiously, right on top of B. Babu's inventing table. 'Now WOT could be the matter?' said B. Babu, as he shot out of his small two-room house into the courtyard. 'Arre, Mohna, Barhna,

Khichri, Motia!' he yelled out to his neighbours, 'Kya ho raha hai bhai?'

And then they heard someone come crashing through the trees towards them. It was Badli, a peon in B. Babu's office. 'Saheb! Some people have been chopping down pilkhan and banyan trees in the forest! And Saheb! The old TIGER who lived in the jungle now has fewer places to hide in and is rushing about frightening the people of Pipli!!' There was confusion at this news and everyone began talking at once, and sounded like a bad orchestra playing nineteen different tunes at the same time. No one wanted to face the tiger of course; they just wanted to be far away from him. Then Khichri came up with a mad idea. He said, 'Babuji! Motia and I will sit here at the edge of the forest and FAST, just like the old sadhus. The POWER of our FASTING will frighten the tiger back into the forest! And then,' added cunning Khichri, 'you can give us a REE-ward, Saheb, like a week's supply of kachoris or even tickets to the movies.'

'Yes yas yas! Oh yas! Please fast fast-fast,' yelled the small crowd of Pipliwallas. Bidesia Babu said, 'OK. It sounds quite cracked, but let's try it.' So Khichri and Motia's families brought them two mats and spread them out a little distance from their huts and quarters, and then they said a little prayer:

Mother Nature
good and kind
Give us brains to
help our minds
We want to calm
down Tigerji
Make sure these
two don't cheat us-ji

'Don't cheat, you two,' said Badli with his hands on his hips, 'if we catch you eating you've had your chips.'

'Arre bhai, don't talk about chips, you're making me hungry,' said Kichri, as Motia gave him a dirty look. After a little while everyone went off to their jobs and household chores and naps. Meanwhile Messrs K. and M. were fasting very hard. When all was silent Motia heard a soft scuffling sound, and turned around to see Khichri trying to stand up quietly. 'Where are you going, Khich?' he asked, and Khich said, 'Oh, just to the, you know, the bathroom.' 'Hokay,' said Motia, and carried on fasting. But of course we know that K. wasn't going to the b-room at ALL. He sprinted off silently to a part of the thicket where there was a guava tree laden with fruit. Shrimaan Kichri ate three juicy guavas, nice big ones, drank some water from a stream nearby and came back looking very innocent. As he sat down he burped, a little tiny burp. Motia opened one eye and said, 'To the bathroom, huh?' and K. said, 'Er, yes yes of course.' Well anyway Motia didn't say anything because he was a peaceful fellow and thought he could chase the tiger away with his own fasting. But he certainly suspected Khichri because as everyone knows no one burps when they come back from the, you know, b–room, they only burp when they've eaten something. For the next two days Khichri disappeared for half an hour each afternoon, and all the while K. was stuffing himself with guavas, poor Motia had been starving, with only a few sips of water to keep him going.

Now friends, on the evening of the third day, just as twilight was beginning to fall, there was the biggest SCENE in Pipli town. Because Tigerji had seen with his keen little eyes our friend Khichri come to sneak guavas for three afternoons, and he also saw there was no one nearby where these two gents were fasting so fast. 'This one looks plump,' he thought, as he saw Khichri on his mat, 'the other's too skinny.' So he crept up silently and then JUST as he LEAPT on top of Khichri, he stopped. Khichri was lying there petrified trying to scream but no voice came out of his throat, he was so terrified. Then he, too, like the Tigerji, heard it. A terrible, horrible sound,

"I'm B. Babu, humble Always at your service-ji! myself Bidesia Babu, very important inventor-ji!"

enough to make even a tiger's hair stand on end. It was a rumbling, grumbling, growling, roaring sound, as if A HUNDRED LIONS were approaching.

'GRROOOAAARRRUMMBLLE,' it went, 'GRRRUMBLE-RUMMBLLERR!!!' Tigerji knew when he was beaten. He couldn't fight a hundred lions. With his eyes still shining like headlights in the twilight, he retreated slowly into the forest, very, very annoyed.

Well, let's all run away fast-fast, you'll say, now that we've got rid of one tiger only to get stuck with a hundred lions. But there was no real need for that. The terrifying rumbling came from dear Motia bhaiya's hungry stomach crying out truthfully for food.

In fact that's what gave Bidesia Babu the idea of The Rumbling Revolver. He had watched the whole thing from his window and was about to aim at Tigerji with a very strong water-hose to chase him away. Then he realized that Motia's honest fasting had given him a wonderful idea for chasing away angry tigers without harming them. Yes! He has made a fine, shiny revolver with a fixture inside which includes a microscopic super-amplifier. The noise it makes resembles that of a huge pride of lions roaring like thunder. And Motia, who is the co-Inventor, has received the wonderful reward of free kachoris for life made by B. Babu's mother.

After this our friend Khichri had to help the people of Pipli replant saplings in the patch which the tree-thieves had cleared, and with the monsoons being so good, the jungle is looking thick and green again. Tigerji has lots of places to hide in now, and the tree-thieves seem to have heard that he's very angry, so they haven't returned.

But Bidesia Babu is busier than ever before. All the Ministers in Delhi want to see his Rumbling Revolver and his Immediate Upstart Finder too, as you will imagine they need it badly because all the upstarts seem to collect in

Delhi. No matter; after all the fame he will have received, Bidesia Babu will still return to Pipli and sing:

I may rumble but
I'm humble
Always at your Íser-
vice-ji!
Myself Bidesia
Babu am
Crackpot   In-
venTORing-ji!

Illustrated by Taposhi Ghoshal

Dhan Gopal Mukerji

•

FROM GAY-NECK: THE STORY OF A PIGEON

After rigorous training and many adventures Gay-Neck and Hira, two Indian carrier-pigeons, are loaned during World War I to the British Army to transmit messages in France. They are accompanied by the wise and knowledgeable hunter Ghond, as their master is under age.

This is Gay-Neck's story, in his own words, of his experiences at the battle-front.

'The next time we were taken to the front was after the Rasseldar recovered from his slight wounds. On this occasion he took both Hira and me. I knew at once that the message we were to carry was so important that two had to be trusted with it so that at least one might succeed.

'It was very cold. I felt as if I were living in a kingdom of ice. It rained all the time. The ground was so foul that every time you stepped on it your feet got caught in mud like quicksand, and your feet felt so cold, as if you had stepped on a corpse.

'Now we reached a strange place. It was not a trench, but a small village. Around it beat and burst the tides of burning destruction. It was, by the look on the men's faces, a very sacred and important place, for they did not want to give it up, though the red tongues of death licked almost every roof, wall and tree of this place. I was very glad to be in an open space. One could see the grey sky low, oh, so very low. And one could see the frost-whited patches of ground where no shell had yet fallen. Even there, in that very heart of pounding and shooting, where houses fell as birds' nests in tempests, rats ran from hole to hole, mice stole cheese, and spiders spun webs to catch flies. They went on with the business of their lives as if the slaughtering of men by their brothers were as negligible as the clouds that covered the sky.

'After a while the booming stopped. And it looked as if the village—that is, what was left of it—were safe from attack. It grew darker and darker. The sky lowered so far that I could put my beak into it. The dank cold seized every feather of my body and began to pull it out, as it were. I found it utterly impossible to sit still in our cage. Hira and I hugged each other tight in order to keep warm.

'Again firing broke out. This time from every direction. Our little village was an island surrounded by the enemy. Apparently under cover of the fog that had enwrapped everything, the enemy had cut off our connection from the rear. Then they started shooting the sky-rockets. It was dark and clammy like a Himalayan night, though it was hardly past noon. I wondered how men knew it was anything but night. Men, after all, know less than birds.

'Hira and I were released to carry our respective messages. We flew up, but not very far, for in a short time we were devoured by a thick fog. Our eyes

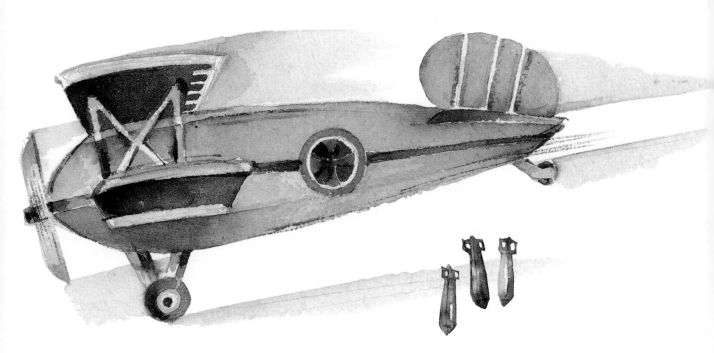

could see nothing. A cold clammy film pressed itself on them, but I had anticipated something like this. I did what I would do under such circumstances, whether on a field of battle or in India. I flew upwards. It seemed as if I could go no farther than a foot at a time. My wings were wet. My breathing was caught in a long process of sneezing. I thought I should drop dead in an instant. Thank the Gods of the pigeons I could see for a few yards now! So I flew higher. Now my eyes began to smart. Suddenly I realized I must draw down my film—my second eyelids that I use in flying through a dust-storm—if I were to save myself from blindness, for we were not in a fog—it was an evil-smelling, eye-destroying smoke let out by men. My eyes pained as if somebody had stuck pins into them. My films now covered my eyes, and, holding my breath, I struggled upwards. Hira, who was accompanying me, rose too. He was choking to death with that gas. But he was not going to give up his flight. At last we rose clear of the sheet of poison smoke. The air was pure here, and as I removed the film from my eyes I saw, far away against the grey sky, our line. We flew towards it.

'Hardly had we flown halfway homeward when a terrible eagle with black crosses all over it flew nearer and spat fire at us—puck puff, puck puff, pop pa... We ducked and did the best we could. We flew back to its rear. There the machine could not hit us. Imagine us flying over the tail of that machine-eagle. It could do nothing. It began to circle. So did we. It turned somersaults. So did we. It could do nothing without wriggling its tail; unlike that of a real eagle, its tail was as stiff as a dead fish. We knew that if we once came in front of it again, we would be killed instantaneously.

'Time was passing. I realized that we could not go on staying over the tail of that machine-eagle for ever. The village covered with poison gas that we had left behind held the Rasseldar and our friends. We must get our message through for their safety and succour.

'Just then the machine-eagle played a trick. It flew

back towards its home. We did not wish to go into the enemy's line flying over its tail in order to be sniped by sharpshooters. Now that we were halfway to our own home and in sight of our line, we gave up being careful; we turned away from the machine-eagle and flew at our highest speed, rising higher every few wing-beats. No sooner had we done that than the miserable beast turned and followed. Fortunately, it took him a little time. There was no doubt now that we were flying over our own lines. Just the same that plane rose to our level and kept on pouring fire on us—puff puff pop pa! Now we were forced to duck and dive. I made Hira fly under me. That protected him. So we flew, but fate is fate. From nowhere came an eagle and fired at the enemy. We felt so safe now that Hira and I flew abreast of each other. Just then a bullet buzzed by me and broke his wings.

Poor wounded Hira! He circled and fell through the air like a silver leaf, fortunately in our line. Seeing that he was dead, I flew at lightning speed, never turning back to see the duel of the two eagles.

'When I got home I was taken to the Commander-in-Chief. He patted my back. Then, for the first time, I realized what an important message I had brought, for as soon as the old man had read the piece of paper he touched some queer ticking things, and he lifted a piece of horn and growled into it. Now Ghond took me to my nest. There, as I perched, thinking of Hira, I felt the very earth shake under me. Machine-eagles flew in the air as thick as locusts. They howled, whirred and barked. Below, from the ground, boomed and groaned innumerable metal dogs. Then came the deep-toned howl of the big spitfires like a whole forest of tigers gone mad. Ghond patted my head and said, "You have saved the day." But there was no day in sight. It was a darkening grey sky under which death coiled and screamed like a dragon, and crushed all in its grip. How bad it was you may gauge from this: when I flew near our base for exercise next morning I found that hardly a mile from my nest the ground was ploughed up by shells. And even rats and field mice did not manage to escape: dozens of them had been slaughtered and cut to pieces. Oh! it was terrible. I felt so melancholy. Now that Hira was dead I was alone, and so weary!'

From the chapter 'Second Adventure'

Illustrated by Pulak Biswas

R. K. Narayan

·

FROM **SWAMI AND FRIENDS**

The location of Swami and Friends *is the town of Malgudi and the year 1930. Spurred by a Swadeshi demonstration, Swaminathan (Swami for short) breaks the windows of Albert Mission School where he studies and has to leave the institution. Swami then joins the Board High School.*

His friends Rajam and Mani decide to put together a cricket team, the MCC.

Work was rather heavy in the Board High School. The amount of homework given at the Albert Mission was nothing compared to the heap given at the Board. Every teacher thought that his was the only subject that the boys had to study. Six sums in Arithmetic, four pages of 'handwriting copy', dictionary meanings of scores of tough words, two maps, and five stanzas in Tamil poetry, were the average homework every day. Swaminathan sometimes wished that he had not left his old school. The teachers here were ruthless beings; not to speak of the drill three evenings a week, there were scout classes, compulsory games, etc. after the regular hours every day; and missing a single class meant half-a-dozen cane cuts on the following day. The wizened spectacled man was a repulsive creature, with his screeching voice; the Head of the Albert Mission had a majestic air about him in spite of all his defects.

All this rigour and discipline resulted in a life with little scope for leisure. Swaminathan got up pretty early, rushed through all his homework, and rose just in time to finish the meal and reach the school as the first bell rang. Every day, as he passed the cloth shop at the end of Market Road, the first bell reached his ears. And just as he panted into the class, the second bell would go off. The bell lacked the rich note of the Albert Mission gong; there was something mean and nasal about it. But he soon got accustomed to it.

Except for an hour in the afternoon, he had to be glued to his seat right till four-thirty in the evening. He had lost the last-bench habit (it might be because he no longer had Mani's company in the classroom). He sat in the second row, and no dawdling easygoing nonsense was tolerated there; you sat right under the teacher's nose. When the four-thirty bell rang, Swaminathan slipped his pencil into his pocket and stretched his cramped aching fingers.

The four-thirty bell held no special thrill. You could not just dash out of the class with a howl of joy. You had to go to the drill ground and stand in a solemn line, and for three-quarters of an hour the Drill Master treated you as if you were his dog. He drove you to march left and right, stand at attention, and swing the arms, or climb the horizontal or parallel bars, whether you liked it or not, whether you knew the thing or not. For aught the Drill Master cared, you might lose your balance on the horizontal bars and crack your skull.

At the end of this you ran home to drink coffee, throw down the books, and rush off to the cricket field, which was a long way off. You covered the distance half running, half walking, moved by the vision of a dun field sparsely covered with scorched grass, lit into a blaze by the slant rays of the evening sun, enveloped in a flimsy cloud of dust, alive with the shouts of players stamping about. What music there was in the thud of the bat hitting the ball! Just as you took the turn leading to Lawley Extension, you looked at the sun, which stood poised like a red-hot coin on the horizon. You hoped it would not sink. But by the time you arrived at the field, the sun went down, leaving only a splash of colour and light in the sky. The shadows already crept out, and one or two municipal lanterns twinkled here and there. You still hoped you would be in time for a good game. But from about half a furlong away you saw the team squatting carelessly round the field. Somebody was wielding the bat rather languidly, bowled and fielded by a handful who were equally languid—the languor that comes at the end of a strenuous evening in the sun.

In addition to the misery of disappointment, you found Rajam a bit sore. He never understood the difficulties of a man. 'Oh, Swami, why are you late again?'

'Wretched drill class.'

'Oh, damn your drill classes and scout classes! Why don't you come early?'

'What can I do, Rajam? I can't help it.'

'Well, well. I don't care. You are always ready with excuses. Since the new bats, balls and things arrived, you have hardly played four times.'

Others being too tired to play, eventually you persuaded the youngest member of the team (a promising, obedient boy of the Fifth Standard, who was admitted because he cringed and begged Rajam perseveringly) to bowl while you batted. And when you tired of it, you asked him to hold the bat and started bowling, and since you were the Tate of the team, the youngster was rather nervous. And again you took up batting, and then bowling, and so on. It went on till it became difficult to find the ball in the semi-darkness and the picker ran after small dark objects on the ground, instead of after the ball. At this stage a rumour started that the ball was lost and caused quite a stir. The figures squatting and reposing got busy, and the ball was retrieved. After this the captain passed an order forbidding further play, and the stumps were drawn for the day, and soon all the players melted in the darkness. You stayed behind with Rajam and Mani, perched upon Rajam's compound wall, and discussed the day's game and the players, noting the improvement, stagnation, or degeneration of each player, till it became quite dark and a peon came to inform Rajam that his tutor had come.

∗∗∗

One evening, returning home from the cricket field, after parting from Mani at the Grove Street junction, Swaminathan's conscience began to trouble him. A slight incident had happened during the early evening when he had gone home from the school to throw down the books and start for the cricket field. He had just thrown down the books and was running towards the kitchen,

when Granny cried, 'Swami, Swami. Oh, boy, come here.'

'No,' he said as usual and was in a moment out of her sight, in the kitchen, violently sucking coffee out of a tumbler. He could still hear her shaky querulous voice calling him. There was something appealing in that weak voice, and he had a fit of pity for her sitting and calling people who paid no heed to her. As soon as he had drunk the coffee, he went to her and asked, 'What do you want?'

She looked up and asked him to sit down. At that he lost his temper and all the tenderness he had felt for her a moment back. He raved, 'If you are going to, say what you have to say as quickly as possible... If not, don't think I am a silly fool...'

She said, 'I shall give you six pies. You can take three pies and bring me a lemon for three pies.' She had wanted to open this question slowly and diplomatically, because she knew what to expect from her grandson. And when she asked him to sit down, she did it as the first diplomatic move.

Without condescending to say yes or no, Swaminathan held out his hand for the coins and took them. Granny said, 'You must come before I count ten.' This imposition of a time limit irritated him. He threw down the coins and said, 'If you want it so urgently, you had better go and get it yourself.' It was nearing five-thirty and he wanted to be in the field before sunset. He stood frowning at her as if giving her the choice of his getting the lemon late when he returned from the field, or not at all. She said, 'I have a terrible pain in the stomach. Please run out and come back, boy.' He did not stay there to hear more.

But now all the excitement and exhilaration of the play being over, and having bidden the last 'goodnight', he stood in the Grove and Vinayak Mudali Street junction, as it were face to face with his soul. He thought of his grandmother and felt guilty. Probably she was writhing with pain at that very moment. It stung his heart as he remembered her pathetic upturned face and watery eyes. He called himself a sneak, a thief, an ingrate, and a hardhearted villain.

In this mood of self-reproach he reached home. He softly sat beside Granny and kept looking at her. It was contrary to his custom. Every evening as soon as he reached home he would dash straight into the kitchen and worry the cook. But now he felt that his hunger did not matter.

Granny's passage had no light. It had only a shaft falling from the lamp in the hall. In the half-darkness, he could not see her face clearly. She lay still. Swaminathan was seized with a horrible passing doubt whether she might not be dead—of stomachache. He controlled his voice and asked, 'Granny, how is your pain?'

Granny stirred, opened her eyes and said, 'Swami, you have come! Have you had your food?'

'Not yet. How is your stomachache, Granny?'

'Oh, it is all right. It is all right.'

It cost him all his mental powers to ask without flinching, 'Did you get the lemon?' He wanted to know it. He had been feeling genuinely anxious about it. Granny answered this question at once, but to Swaminathan it seemed an age— a terrible stretch of time during which anything might happen, she might say anything, scold him, disown him, swear that she would have nothing more to do with him, or say reproachfully that if only he had cared to go and purchase the lemon in time he might have saved her, and that she was going to die in a few minutes. But she simply said, 'You did right in not going. Your mother had kept a dozen in the kitchen.'

Swaminathan was overjoyed to hear this good news. And he expressed this mood of joy in: 'You know what my new name is? I am Tate.'

'What?'

'Tate.'

'What is Tate?' she asked innocently. Swaminathan's disappointment was twofold: she had not known anything of his new title, and failed to understand its rich significance even when told. At other times he would have shouted at her. But now he was a fresh penitent, and so asked her kindly, 'Do you mean to say that you don't know Tate?'

'I don't know what you mean.'

'Tate, the great cricket player, the greatest bowler on earth. I hope you know what cricket is.'

'What is that?' Granny asked. Swaminathan was aghast at this piece of illiteracy. 'Do you mean to say, Granny, that you don't know what cricket is, or are you fooling me?'

'I don't know what you mean.'

'Don't keep on saying "I don't know what you mean". I wonder what the boys and men of your days did in the evenings! I think they spent all the twenty-four hours in doing holy things.'

He considered for a second. Here was his Granny stagnating in appalling ignorance; and he felt it his duty to save her. He delivered a short speech setting forth the principles, ideals, and the philosophy of the game of cricket, mentioning the radiant gods of that world. He asked her every few seconds if she understood, and she nodded her head, though she caught only three per cent of what he said. He concluded the speech with a sketch of the history and the prospects of the MCC. 'But for Rajam, Granny,' he said, 'I

don't know where we should have been. He has spent hundreds of rupees on this team. Buying bats and balls is no joke. He has plenty of money in his box. Our team is known even to the Government. If you like, you may write a letter to the MCC and it will be delivered to us promptly. You will see us winning all the cups in Malgudi, and in course of time we shall show even the Madras fellows what cricket is.' He added a very important note: 'Don't imagine all sorts of fellows can become players in our team.'

His father stood behind him, with the baby in his arms. He asked, 'What are you lecturing about, young man?'

Swaminathan had not noticed his father's presence, and now writhed awkwardly as he answered, 'Nothing...Oh, nothing, Father.'

'Come on. Let me know it too.'

'It is nothing—Granny wanted to know something about cricket and I was explaining it to her.'

'Indeed! I never knew Mother was a sportswoman. Mother, I hope Swami has filled you with cricket-wisdom.'

Granny said, 'Don't tease the boy. The child is so fond of me. Poor thing! He has been trying to tell me all sorts of things. You are not in the habit of explaining things to me. You are all big men...'

Father replied, pointing at the baby, 'Just wait a few days and this little fellow will teach you all the philosophy and the politics in the world.' He gently clouted the baby's fat cheeks, and the baby gurgled and chirped joyfully. 'He has already started lecturing. Listen attentively, Mother.' Granny held up her arms for the baby. But Father clung to him tight and said, 'No. No. I came home early only for this fellow's sake. I can't. Come on, Swami, I think we had better sit down for food. Where is your mother?'

***

The captain sternly disapproved of Swaminathan's ways. 'Swami, I must warn you. You are neglecting the game. You are not having any practice at all.'

'It is this wretched Board School work.'

'Who asked you to go and join it? They never came and invited you. Never mind. But let me tell you. Even Bradman, Tate, and everybody spends four to five hours on the pitch every day, practising, practising. Do you think you are greater than they?'

'Captain, listen to me. I do my best to arrive at the field before five. But this wretched Board High School timetable is peculiar.'

A way out had to be found. The captain suggested, 'You must see your headmaster and ask him to exempt you from extra work till the match is over.' It was more easily said than done, and Swaminathan said so, conjuring up before his mind a picture of the wizened face and the small dingy spectacles of his headmaster.

'I am afraid to ask that monster,' Swaminathan said. 'He may detain me in Second Form for ages.'

'Indeed! Are you telling me that you are in such terror of your headmaster? Suppose I see him?'

'Oh, please don't, Captain. I beg you. You don't know what a vicious being he is. He may not treat you well. Even if he behaves well before you, he is sure to kill me when you are gone.'

'What is the matter with you, Swami? Your head is full of nonsense. How are we to go on? It is two months since we started the team, and you have not played even for ten days...'

Mani, who had stretched himself on the compound wall, now broke in: 'Let us see what your headmaster can do. Let him say yes or no. If he kills you I will pulp him. My clubs have had no work for a long time.'

There was no stopping Rajam. The next day he insisted that he would see the headmaster at the school. He would not mind losing a couple of periods of his own class. Mani offered to go with him but was advised to mind his business.

Next morning at nine-thirty Swaminathan spent five minutes rubbing his eyes red, and then complained of headache. His father felt his temples and said that he would be all right if he dashed a little cold water on his forehead.

'Yes, Father,' Swaminathan said and went out. He stood outside Father's room and decided that if cold water was a cure for headache he would avoid it, since he was praying for that malady just then. Rajam was coming to see the headmaster, and it would be unwise to go to school that morning. He went in and asked, 'Father, did you say cold water?'

'Yes.'

'But don't you think it will give me pneumonia or something? I am also feeling feverish.'

Father felt his pulse and said, 'Now run to school and you will be all right.' It was easier to squeeze milk out of a stone than to get permission from Father to keep away from school.

He whispered into his Granny's ear, 'Granny, even if I die, I am sure Father will insist on sending my corpse to the school.' Granny protested vehemently against this sentiment.

'Granny, a terrible fever is raging within me and my head is splitting with headache. But yet, I mustn't keep away from school.'

Granny said, 'Don't go to school.' She then called Mother and said, 'This child has fever. Why should he go to school?'

'Has he?' Mother asked anxiously, and fussed over him. She felt his body and said that he certainly had a temperature. Swaminathan said pathetically, 'Give me milk or something, Mother. It is getting late for school.' Mother vetoed this virtuous proposal. Swaminathan faintly said, 'But Father may not like it.' She asked him to lie down on a bed and hurried along to Father's room. She stepped into the room with the declaration, 'Swami has fever, and he can't go to school.'

'Did you take his temperature?'

'Not yet. It doesn't matter if he misses the school for a day.'

'Anyway, take his temperature,' he said. He feared that his wife might detect the sarcasm in his suggestion, and added as a palliative, 'That we may know whether a doctor is necessary.'

A thermometer stuck out of Swaminathan's mouth for half a minute and indicated normal. Mother looked at it and thrust it back into his mouth. It again showed normal. She took it to Father, and he said, 'Well, it is normal,' itching to add, 'I knew it.' Mother insisted, 'Something has gone wrong with the thermometer. The boy has fever. There is no better thermometer than my hand. I can swear that he has 100.2 now.'

'Quite likely,' Father said.

And Swaminathan, when he ought to have been at school, was lying peacefully, with closed eyes, on his bed. He heard a footstep near his bed and opened his eyes. Father stood over him and said in an undertone, 'You are a lucky fellow. What a lot of champions you have in this house when you don't want to go to school!' Swaminathan felt that this was a sudden and unprovoked attack from behind. He shut his eyes and turned towards the wall with a feeble groan.

By the afternoon he was already bedsore. He dreaded the prospect of staying in bed through the evening. Moreover, Rajam would have already come to the school in the morning and gone.

He went to his mother and informed her that he was starting for the school. There was a violent protest at once. She felt him all over and said that he was certainly better but in no condition to go to school. Swaminathan said, 'I am feeling quite fit, Mother. Don't get fussy.'

On the way to the school he met Rajam and Mani. Mani had his club under his arm. Swaminathan feared that these two had done something serious.

Rajam said, 'You are a fine fellow! Where were you this morning?'

'Did you see the headmaster, Rajam?'

'Not yet. I found that you had not come, and did not see him. I want you to be with me when I see him. After all it is your business.'

When Swaminathan emerged from the emotional chaos which followed Rajam's words, he asked, 'What is Mani doing here?'

'I don't know,' Rajam said. 'I found him outside your school with his club, when he ought to have been in his class.'

'Mani, what about your class?'

'It is all right,' Mani replied, 'I didn't attend it today.'

'And why your club?' Swaminathan asked.

'Oh! I simply brought it along.'

Rajam asked, 'Weren't you told yesterday to attend your class and mind your business?'

'I don't remember. You asked me to mind my business only when I offered to accompany you. I am not accompanying you. I just came this way, and you have also come this way. This is a public road.' Mani's jest was lost on them.

Their minds were too busy with plans for the impending interview.

'Don't worry, young men,' Mani said. 'I shall see you through your troubles. I will talk to the headmaster, if you like.'

'If you step into his room, he will call the police,' Swaminathan said.

When they reached the school, Mani was asked to go away, or at worst wait on the road. Rajam went in, and Swaminathan was compelled to accompany him to the headmaster's room.

The headmaster was sleeping with his head between his hands and his elbows resting on the table. It was a small stuffy room with only one window opening on the weather-beaten side-wall of a shop; it was cluttered with dust-laden rolls of maps, globes, and geometrical squares. The headmaster's white cane lay on the table across two ink bottles and some pads. The sun came in a hot dusty beam and fell on the headmaster's nose and the table. He was gently snoring. This was a possibility that Rajam had not thought of.

'What shall we do?' Swaminathan asked in a rasping whisper.

'Wait,' Rajam ordered.

They waited for ten minutes and

then began to make gentle noises with their feet. The headmaster opened his eyes and without taking his head from his hands, kept staring at them vacantly, without showing any sign of recognition. He rubbed his eyes, raised his eyebrows three times, yawned, and asked in a voice thick with sleep, 'Have you fellows no class?' He fumbled for his spectacles and put them on. Now the picture was complete—wizened face and dingy spectacles calculated to strike terror into the hearts of Swaminathans. He asked again, 'To what class do you fellows belong? Have you no class?'

'I don't belong to your school,' Rajam said defiantly.

'Ah, then which heaven do you drop from?'

Rajam said, 'I am the captain of the MCC and have come to see you on business.'

'What is that?'

'This is my friend W.S. Swaminathan of Second C studying in your school...'

'I am honoured to meet you,' said the headmaster turning to Swaminathan. Rajam felt at that moment that he had found out where the Board High School got its reputation from.

'I am the captain of the MCC.'

'Equally honoured...'

'He is in my team. He is a good bowler...'

'Are you?' said the headmaster, turning to Swaminathan.

'May I come to the point?' Rajam asked.

'Do, do,' said the headmaster, 'for heaven's sake, do.'

'It is this,' Rajam said, 'he is a good bowler and he needs some practice. He can't come to the field early enough because he is kept in the school every day after four-thirty.'

'What do you want me to do?'

'Sir, can't you permit him to go home after four-thirty?'

The headmaster sank back in his chair and remained silent.

Rajam asked again, 'What do you say, sir, won't you do it?'

'Are you the headmaster of this school or am I?'

'Of course you are the headmaster, sir. In Albert Mission they don't keep us a minute longer than four-thirty. And we are exempted from drill if we play games.'

'Here I am not prepared to listen to your rhapsodies on that pariah school. Get out.'

Mani, who had been waiting outside, finding his friends gone too long, and having his own fears, now came into the headmaster's room.

'Who is this?' asked the headmaster, looking at Mani sourly. 'What do you want?'

'Nothing,' Mani replied and quietly stood in a corner.

'I can't understand why every fellow who finds nothing to do comes and stands in my room.'

'I am the Police Superintendent's son,' Rajam said abruptly.

'Is that so? Find out from your father what he was doing on the day a gang of little rascals came in and smashed these windows... What is the thing that fellow has in his hand?'

'My wooden club,' Mani answered.

Rajam added, 'He breaks skulls with it. Come out, Mani, come on, Swami. There is nothing doing with this—this madcap.'

From the chapter 'Granny Shows Her Ignorance'

Illustrated by Niren Sen Gupta

Premchand

·

FESTIVAL OF EID

A full thirty days after Ramadan comes Eid. How wonderful and beautiful is the morning of Eid! The trees look greener, the fields more festive, the sky has a lovely pink glow. Look at the sun! It comes up brighter and more dazzling than before to wish the world a very happy Eid.

The village is agog with excitement. Everyone is up early to go to the Eidgah mosque which is a good three miles from the village.

The boys are more excited than the others. Some of them kept only one fast—and that only till noon. Some didn't even do that. But no one can deny them the joy of going to the Eidgah. Fasting is for the grown-ups and the aged. For the boys it is only the day of Eid. They have been talking about it all the time. At long last the day has come. And now they are impatient with people for not hurrying up. They have no concern with things that have to be done. They are not bothered whether or not there is enough milk and sugar for the vermicelli pudding. All they want is to eat the pudding. They have no idea why Abbajan is out of breath running to the house of Chaudhri Karim Ali. They don't know that if the Chaudhri were to change his mind he could turn the festive day of Eid into a day of mourning. Their pockets bulge with coins like the stomach of the pot-bellied Kubera, the Hindu God of Wealth. They are forever taking the treasure out of their pockets, counting and recounting it before putting it back. Mahmood counts 'One, two, ten, twelve'—he has twelve pice. Mohsin has 'One, two, three, eight, nine, fifteen' pice. Out of this countless hoard they will buy countless things: toys, sweets, paper-pipes, rubber balls—and much else.

The happiest of the boys is Hamid. He is only four, poorly dressed, thin and famished-looking. His father died last year of cholera. Then his mother wasted away and, without anyone finding out what had ailed her she also died. Now Hamid sleeps in Granny Ameena's lap and is as happy as a lark. She tells him that his father has gone to earn money and will return with sackloads of silver. And that his mother has gone to Allah to get lovely gifts for him. This makes Hamid very happy. It is great to live on hope.

Hamid has no shoes on his feet; the cap on his head is soiled and tattered; its gold thread has turned black. Nevertheless Hamid is happy. He knows that when his father comes back with sacks full of silver and his mother with gifts from Allah he will be able to fulfil all his heart's desires. Then he will have more than Mahmood, Mohsin, Noorey and Sammi.

In her hovel the unfortunate Ameena sheds bitter tears. It is Eid and she does not have even a handful of grain. Only if her Abid were there, it would have been a different kind of Eid!

Hamid goes to his grandmother and says, 'Granny, don't you fret over me! I will be the first to get back. Don't worry!'

Ameena is sad. Other boys are going out with their fathers. She is the only 'father' Hamid has. How can she let him go to the fair all by himself? What if he gets lost in the crowd? No, she must not lose her precious little soul! How can he walk three miles? He doesn't even have a pair of shoes. He will get blisters on his feet. If she went along with him she could pick him up now and then. But then who would be there to cook the vermicelli? If only she had the money she could have bought the ingredients on the way back and quickly made the pudding. In the village it would take her many hours to get everything. The only way out was to ask someone for them.

The villagers leave in one party. With the boys is Hamid. They run on ahead of the elders and wait for them under a tree. Why do the oldies drag their feet? And Hamid is like one with wings on his feet. How could anyone think he would get tired?

They reach the suburbs of the town. On both sides of the road are mansions of the rich enclosed all around by thick, high walls. In the gardens mango and litchi trees are laden with fruit. A boy hurls a stone at a mango tree. The gardener rushes out screaming abuses at them. By then the boys are a furlong out of his reach and roaring with laughter.

Then come big buildings: the law courts, the college and the club. How many boys would there be in this big college? No sir, they are not all boys! Some are grown-up men. They sport enormous moustaches. What are such grown-up men going on studying for? And the white folk play games in the evenings. Grown-up men, men with moustaches and beards playing games! And not only they, but even their Memsahibs! That's the honest truth! You give my Granny that something they call a racket; she wouldn't know how to hold it. And if she tried to wave it about she would collapse.

Mahmood says, 'My mother's hands would shake; I swear by Allah they would!'

Mohsin says, 'Mine can grind maunds of grain. Her hand would never shake holding a miserable racket. She draws hundreds of pitchers full of water from the well every day. My buffalo drinks up five pitchers. If a Memsahib had to draw one pitcher, she would go blue in the face.'

Mahmood interrupts, 'But your mother couldn't run and leap about, could she?'

'That's right,' replies Mohsin, 'she couldn't leap or jump. But one day our cow got loose and began grazing in the Chaudhri's fields. My mother ran so fast after it that I couldn't catch up with her. Honest to God, I could not!'

So we proceed to the stores of the sweetmeat vendors. All so gaily decorated! Who can eat all these delicacies? Just look! Every store has them piled up in mountain heaps. They say that after nightfall, Jinns come and buy up everything. 'My Abba says that at midnight there is a Jinn at every stall. He has all that remains weighed and pays in real rupees, just the sort of rupees we have,' says Mohsin.

Hamid is not convinced. 'Where would the Jinns come by rupees?'

'Jinns are never short of money,' replies Mohsin. 'They can get into any treasury they want. Mister, don't you know no iron bars can stop them? They have all the diamonds and rubies they want. If they are pleased with anyone they will give him baskets full of diamonds. They are here one moment and five minutes later they can be in Calcutta.'

Hamid asks again, 'Are these Jinns very big?'

'Each one is as big as the sky,' asserts Mohsin. 'He has his feet on the ground, his head touches the sky. But if he so wanted, he could get into a tiny brass pot.'

'How do people make Jinns happy?' asks Hamid. 'If anyone taught me the secret, I would make at least one Jinn happy with me.'

'I do not know,' replies Mohsin, 'but the Chaudhri Sahib has a lot of Jinns under his control. If anything is stolen, he can trace it and even tell you the name of the thief. Jinns tell him everything that is going on in the world.'

Hamid understands how Chaudhri Sahib has come by his wealth and why people hold him in so much respect.

It begins to get crowded. Parties heading for the Eidgah are coming into town from different sides—each one dressed better than the other. Some on tongas and ekkas; some in motor cars. All wearing perfume; all bursting with excitement. Our small party of villagers is not bothered about the poor show they make. They are a calm, contented lot.

For village children everything in the town is strange. Whatever catches their eye, they stand and gape at it with wonder. Cars hoot frantically to get them out of the way, but they couldn't care less. Hamid is nearly run over by a car.

At long last the Eidgah comes in view. Above it are massive tamarind trees casting their shade on the cemented floor on which carpets have been spread.

And there are row upon row of worshippers as far as the eye can see, spilling well beyond the mosque courtyard. Newcomers line themselves behind the others. Here neither wealth nor status matter because in the eyes of Islam all men are equal. Our villagers wash their hands and feet and make their own line behind the others. What a beautiful, heart-moving sight it is! What perfect coordination of movements! A hundred thousand heads bow together in prayer! And then all together they stand erect; bow down and sit on their knees! Many times they repeat these movements—exactly as if a hundred thousand electric bulbs were switched on and off at the same time again and again. What a wonderful spectacle it is!

The prayer is over. Men embrace each other. They descend on the sweet and toy-vendors' stores like an army moving to an assault. In this matter the grown-ups are no less eager than the boys. Look, here is a swing! Pay a pice and enjoy riding up to the heavens and then plummeting down to the earth. And here is the roundabout strung with wooden elephants, horses and camels! Pay one pice and have twenty-five rounds of fun. Mahmood and Mohsin and Noorey and other boys mount the horses and camels.

Hamid watches them from a distance. All he has are three pice. He couldn't afford to part with a third of his treasure for a few miserable rounds.

They've finished with the roundabouts; now it is time for the toys. There is a row of stalls on one side with all kinds of toys; soldiers and milkmaids, kings and ministers, water-carriers and washer-women and holy men. Splendid display! How lifelike! All they need are tongues to speak. Mahmood buys a policeman in khaki with a red turban on his head and a gun on his shoulder. Looks as if he is marching in a parade. Mohsin likes the water-carrier with his back bent under the weight of the waterbag. He holds the handle of the bag in one hand and looks pleased with himself. Perhaps he is singing. It seems as if the water is about to pour out of the bag. Noorey has fallen for the lawyer. What an expression of learning he has on his face! A black gown over a long, white coat with a gold watch chain going into a pocket, a fat volume of some law book in his hand. Appears as if he has just finished arguing a case in a court of law.

These toys cost two pice each. All Hamid has are three pice; how can he afford to buy such expensive toys? If they dropped out of his hand, they would be smashed to bits. If a drop of water fell on them, the paint would run. What would he do with toys like these? They'd be of no use to him.

Mohsin says, 'My water-carrier will sprinkle water every day, morning and evening.'

Mahmood says, 'My policeman will guard my house. If a thief comes near, he will shoot him with his gun.'

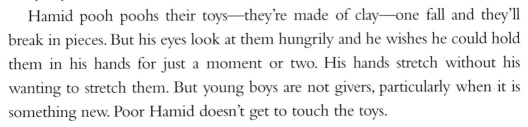

Noorey says, 'My lawyer will fight my cases.'

Sammi says, 'My washer-woman will wash my clothes every day.'

Hamid pooh poohs their toys—they're made of clay—one fall and they'll break in pieces. But his eyes look at them hungrily and he wishes he could hold them in his hands for just a moment or two. His hands stretch without his wanting to stretch them. But young boys are not givers, particularly when it is something new. Poor Hamid doesn't get to touch the toys.

After the toys, it is sweets. Someone buys sesame-seed candy, others gulab jamuns or halva. They smack their lips with relish. Only Hamid is left out. The luckless boy has at least three pice; why doesn't he also buy something to eat? He looks with hungry eyes at the others.

Mohsin says, 'Hamid, take this sesame candy, it smells good.'

Hamid suspects it is a cruel joke; he knows Mohsin doesn't have so big a heart. But knowing this Hamid goes to Mohsin. Mohsin takes a piece out of his leaf-wrap and holds it towards Hamid. Hamid stretches out his hand. Mohsin puts the candy in his own mouth. Mahmood, Noorey and Sammi clap their hands with glee and have a good laugh. Hamid is crestfallen.

Mohsin says, 'This time I will let you have it. I swear by Allah! I will give it to you. Come and take it.'

Hamid replies, 'You keep your sweets. Don't I have money?'

'All you have are three pice,' says Sammi. 'What can you buy for three pice?'

Mahmood says, 'Mohsin is a rascal. Hamid you come to me and I will give you gulab jamuns.'

Hamid replies, 'What is there to rave about sweets? Books are full of bad things about eating sweets.'

'In your heart you must be saying: "If I could get it I would eat it,"' says Mohsin. 'Why don't you take the money out of your pocket?'

'I know what this clever fellow is up to,' says Mahmood. 'When we've spent all our money, he will buy sweets and tease us.'

After the sweet vendors there are a few hardware stores and shops of real and artificial jewellery. There is nothing there to attract the boys' attention. So they go ahead—all of them except Hamid who stops to see a pile of tongs. It occurs to him that his granny does not have a pair of tongs. Each time she bakes chappatis, the iron plate burns her hands. If he were to buy her a pair of tongs she would be very pleased. She would never burn her fingers; they would be a useful thing to have in the house. What use are toys? They are a waste of money. You can have some fun with them but only for a very short time. Then you forget all about them.

Hamid's friends have gone ahead. They are at a stall drinking sherbet. How selfish they are! They bought so many sweets but did not give him one. And then they want him to play with them; they want him to do odd jobs for them. Now if any of them asked him to do something, he would tell them, 'Go suck your lollipop, it will burn your mouth; it will give you a rash of pimples and boils; your tongue will always crave for sweets; you will have to steal money to buy them and get a thrashing in the bargain. It's all written in books. Nothing will happen to my tongs. No sooner my granny sees my pair of tongs than she will run up to take them from me and say, "My child has brought me a pair of tongs", and shower me with a thousand blessings. She will show them off to the neighbours' womenfolk. Soon the whole village will be saying, "Hamid has brought his granny a pair of tongs, how nice he is!" No one will bless the other boys for the toys they have got for themselves. Blessings of elders are heard in the court of Allah and are immediately acted on. Because I have no money Mohsin and Mahmood adopt such airs towards me. I will teach them a lesson. Let them play with their toys and eat all the sweets they can. I will not play with toys. I will not stand any nonsense from anyone. And one day my father will return. And also my mother. Then I will ask these chaps, "Do you want any toys? How many?" I will give each one a basket full of toys and teach them how to treat friends. I am not the sort who buys a pice worth of lollipops to tease others by sucking them myself. I know they will laugh and say Hamid has brought a pair of tongs. They can go to the Devil!'

Hamid asks the shopkeeper, 'How much for this pair of tongs?'

The shopkeeper looks at him and seeing no older person with him replies, 'They're not for you.'

'Are they for sale or not?'

'Why should they not be for sale? Why else should I have bothered to bring them here?'

'Why then don't you tell me how much they are?'

'They will cost you six pice.'

Hamid's heart sinks. 'Let me have the correct price.'

'All right, five pice, bottom price. Take it or leave it.' Hamid steels his heart and says, 'Will you give them to me for three?' And proceeds to walk away lest the shopkeeper screams at him. But the shopkeeper does not scream. On the contrary, he calls Hamid back and gives him the pair of tongs. Hamid carries them on his shoulder as if the tongs were a gun and struts up proudly to show them to his friends. Let us hear what they have to say.

Mohsin laughs and says, 'Are you crazy? What will you do with the tongs?'

Hamid flings the tongs on the ground and replies, 'Try and throw your water-carrier on the ground. Every bone in his body will break.'

Mahmood says, 'Are these tongs some kind of toy?'

'Why not?' retorts Hamid. 'Place them across your shoulders and it is a gun; wield them in your hands and it is like the tongs carried by singing mendicants—they can make the same clanging as a pair of cymbals. One smack and they will reduce all your toys to dust. And much as your toys may try they could not bend a hair on the head of my tongs. My tongs are like a brave tiger.'

Sammi who had bought a small tambourine asks, 'Will you exchange them for my tambourine? It is worth eight pice.'

Hamid pretends not to look at the tambourine. 'My tongs if they wanted to could tear out the bowels of your tambourine. All it has is a leather skin and all it can say is dhub, dhub. A drop of water could silence it forever. My brave pair of tongs can weather water and storms, without budging an inch.'

The pair of tongs wins over everyone to its side. But now no one has any money left and the fairground has been left far behind. It is well past 9 a.m. and the sun is getting hotter every minute. Everyone is in a hurry to get home. Even if they talked their fathers into it, they could not get the tongs. This Hamid is a bit of a rascal. He saved up his money for the tongs.

The boys divide into two factions. Mohsin, Mahmood, Sammi and Noorey on the one side, and Hamid by himself on the other. They are engaged in hot argument. Sammi has defected to the other side. But Mohsin, Mahmood and Noorey, though they are a year or two older than Hamid, are reluctant to take him on in debate. Right is on Hamid's side. Also it's moral force on the one side, clay on the other. Hamid has iron now calling itself steel, unconquerable and lethal. If a tiger was to spring on them the water-carrier would be out of his wits; Mister Constable would drop his clay gun and take to his heels; the lawyer would hide his face in his gown, lie down on the ground and wail as if his mother's mother had died. But the tongs, the pair of tongs, Champion of India would leap and grab the tiger by its neck and gouge out its eyes.

Mohsin puts all he has in his plea, 'But they cannot go and fetch water, can they?'

Hamid raises the tongs and replies, 'One angry word of command from my tongs and your water-carrier will hasten to fetch the water and sprinkle it at any doorstep he is ordered to.'

Mohsin has no answer. Mahmood comes to his rescue. 'If we are caught, we are caught. We will have to do the rounds of the law courts in chains. Then we will be at the lawyer's feet asking for help.'

Hamid has no answer to this powerful argument. He asks, 'Who will come to arrest us?'

Noorey puffs out his chest and replies, 'This policeman with the gun.'

Hamid makes a face and says with scorn, 'This wretch come to arrest the Champion of India! Okay, let's have it out over a bout of wrestling. Far from catching them, he will be scared to look at my tongs in the face.'

Mohsin thinks of another ploy. 'Your tongs' face will burn in the fire every day.' He is sure that this will leave Hamid speechless. That is not so. Pat comes Hamid with the retort, 'Mister, it is only the brave who can jump into a fire. Your miserable lawyers, policemen, and water-carriers will run like frightened women into their homes. Only this Champion of India can perform this feat of leaping into the fire.'

Mahmood has one more try. 'The lawyer will have chairs to sit and tables for his things. Your tongs will only have the kitchen floor to lie on.'

Hamid cannot think of an appropriate retort so he says whatever comes into his mind, 'The tongs won't stay in the kitchen. When your lawyer sits on his chair my tongs will knock him down on the ground.'

It does not make sense but our three heroes are utterly squashed—almost as if a champion kite had been brought down from the heavens to the earth by a cheap, miserable paper imitation. Thus Hamid wins the field. His tongs are the Champion of India. Neither Mohsin nor Mahmood, neither Noorey nor Sammi—nor anyone else can dispute the fact.

The respect that a victor commands from the vanquished is paid to Hamid. The others have spent between twelve to sixteen pice each and bought nothing worthwhile. Hamid's three-pice worth has carried the day. And no one can deny that toys are unreliable things: they break, while Hamid's tongs will remain as they are for years.

The boys begin to make terms of peace. Mohsin says, 'Give me your tongs for a while, you can have my water-carrier for the same time.'

Both Mahmood and Noorey similarly offer their toys. Hamid has no hesitation in agreeing to these terms. The tongs pass from one hand to another; and the toys are in turn handed to Hamid. How lovely they are!

Hamid tries to wipe the tears of his defeated adversaries. 'I was simply pulling your leg, honestly I was. How can these tongs made of iron compare with your toys?' It seems that one or the other will call Hamid's bluff. But Mohsin's party are not solaced. The tongs have won the day and no amount of water can wash away their stamp of authority. Mohsin says, 'No one will bless us for these toys.'

Mahmood adds, 'You talk of blessings! We may get a thrashing instead. My Amma is bound to say, "Are these earthen toys all that you could find at the fair?"'

Hamid has to concede that no mother will be as pleased with the toys as his granny will be when she sees the tongs. All he had was three pice and he has no reason to regret the way he has spent them. And now his tongs are the Champion of India and king of toys.

By eleven the village was again agog with excitement. All those who had gone to the fair were back at home. Mohsin's little sister ran up, wrenched the water-carrier out of his hands and began to dance with joy. Mister Water-

Carrier slipped out of her hand, fell on the ground and went to paradise. The brother and sister began to fight; and both had lots to cry about. Their mother lost her temper because of the racket they were making and gave each two resounding slaps.

Noorey's lawyer met an end befitting his grand status. A lawyer could not sit on the ground. He had to keep his dignity in mind. Two nails were driven into the wall, a plank put on them and a carpet of paper spread on the plank. The honourable counsel was seated like a king on his throne. Noorey began to wave a fan over him. He knew that in the law courts there were khus curtains and electric fans. So the least he could do was to provide a hand fan, otherwise the hot legal arguments might affect his lawyer's brains. Noorey was waving his fan made of bamboo leaf. We do not know whether it was the breeze or the fan or something else that brought the honourable counsel down from his high pedestal to the depths of hell and reduced his gown to the dust of which it was made. There was much beating of breasts and the lawyer's bier was dumped on a dung heap.

Mahmood's policeman remained. He was immediately put on duty to guard the village. But this police constable was no ordinary mortal who could walk on his own two feet. He had to be provided a palanquin. This was a basket lined with tatters of discarded clothes of red colour for the policeman to recline in comfort. Mahmood picked up the basket and started on his rounds. His two younger brothers followed him lisping, 'Shleepers, keep awake!' But night has to be dark; Mahmood stumbled, the basket slipped out of his hand. Mr Constable with his gun crashed on the ground. He was short of one leg. Mahmood being a bit of a doctor knew of an ointment which could quickly rejoin broken limbs. All it needed was the milk of a banyan sapling. The milk was brought and the broken leg reassembled. But no sooner was the constable put on his feet, the leg gave way. One leg was of no use because now he could neither walk nor sit. Mahmood became a surgeon and cut the other leg to the size of the broken one so the chap could at least sit in comfort.

The constable was made into a holy man; he could sit in one place and guard the village. And sometimes he was like the image of the deity. The plume on his turban was scraped off and you could make as many changes in his appearance as you liked. And sometimes he was used for nothing better than weighing things.

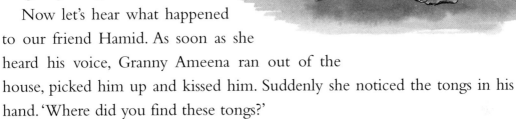

Now let's hear what happened to our friend Hamid. As soon as she heard his voice, Granny Ameena ran out of the house, picked him up and kissed him. Suddenly she noticed the tongs in his hand. 'Where did you find these tongs?'

'I bought them.'

'How much did you pay for them?'

'Three pice.'

Granny Ameena beat her breast. 'You are a stupid child! It is almost noon and you haven't had anything to eat or drink. And what do you buy—tongs! Couldn't you find anything better in the fair than this pair of iron tongs?'

Hamid replied in injured tones, 'You burn your fingers on the iron plate. That is why I bought them.'

The old woman's temper suddenly changed to love—not the kind of calculated love which wastes away in spoken words. This love was mute, solid and seeped with tenderness. What a selfless child! What concern for others! What a big heart! How he must have suffered seeing other boys buying toys and gobbling sweets! How was he able to suppress his own feelings! Even at the fair he thought of his old grandmother. Granny Ameena's heart was too full for words.

And the strangest thing happened—stranger than the part played by the tongs was the role of Hamid the child playing Hamid the old man. And old Granny Ameena became Ameena the little girl. She broke down. She spread her apron and beseeched Allah's blessings for her grandchild. Big tears fell from her eyes. How was Hamid to understand what was going on inside her!

Translated from the Hindi by Khushwant Singh

Illustrated by Jagdish Joshi

Shanta Rameshwar Rao

· ———

THE CONCERT

One morning, in a small apartment in Bombay a girl of about sixteen looked up from the newspaper and said excitedly, 'Pandit Ravi Shankar's playing tomorrow at the Shanmukhananda auditorium.'

'Sh-sh,' said her mother pointing to the figure sleeping on the bed. 'You'll wake him up. You know he needs all the sleep and rest he can get.'

But the boy on the bed was not asleep. 'Pandit Ravi Shankar!' he said. 'Pandit Ravi Shankar, the sitar maestro?' He raised himself up on his elbows for one second, then fell back. But his eyes were shining. 'We mustn't miss the chance,' he said. 'I've—I've—always wanted to hear him and see him...'

'Lie down son, lie down.' His mother sprang to his side. 'He actually raised himself up without help,' she murmured with a catch in her throat and her eyes turned to the idols on a corner shelf. The prayer, which she uttered endlessly, came unbidden to her lips.

'I must hear him and see him,' the boy repeated. 'It's the chance of a lifetime.' Then he began to cough and gasp for breath and had to be given oxygen from the cylinder that stood under the bed. But his large eyes were fixed on his sister.

Smita bit her lip in self-reproach. She had been so excited at seeing the announcement that she had not remembered that her brother was very ill. She had seen how the doctors had shaken their heads gravely and spoken words that neither she nor even her parents could understand. But somewhere deep inside Smita had known the frightening truth—that Anant was going to die. The word *cancer* had hung in the air—her brother was dying of cancer even though she pretended that all would be well and they would return together, a small family of four, to their home in Gaganpur. And he was only fifteen, and the best table-tennis player in the school and the fastest runner. He was learning to play the sitar; they were both taking sitar lessons, but Anant was better than her as in many other things. He was already able to compose his own tunes to the astonishment of their guru. Then cancer had struck and they had come to Bombay so that he could be treated at the cancer hospital in the city.

Whenever they came to Bombay they stayed with Aunt Sushila. Her apartment was not big but there was always room for them.

They had come with high hopes in the miracles of modern science. They told themselves that Anant would be cured at the hospital and he would again walk and run and even take part in the forthcoming table-tennis tournament. And, he would play the sitar—perhaps be a great sitarist one day. But his condition grew worse with each passing day and the doctors at the cancer hospital said, 'Take him home. Give him the things he likes, indulge him,' and they knew then that the boy had not many days to live. But they did not voice their fears. They laughed and smiled and talked and surrounded Anant with whatever made him happy. They fulfilled his every need and gave him whatever he asked for. And now he was asking to go to the concert. 'The chance of a lifetime,' he was saying.

'When you are better,' his mother said. 'This is not the last time they are going to play.'

Smita stood at the window looking at the traffic, her eyes wet with tears. Her mother whispered, 'But you Smita, you must go. Your father will take you.'

When she was alone with Aunt Sushila, Smita cried out in a choked voice, 'No, how can I? We've always done things together, Anant and I.'

'A walk in the park might make you feel better,' said Aunt Sushila and Smita was grateful for her suggestion.

In the park, people were walking, running, playing ball, doing yogic exercises, feeding the ducks and eating roasted gram and peanuts. Smita felt alone in their midst. She was lost in her thoughts.

Suddenly a daring thought came to her and as she hurried home she said to herself, 'Why not? There's no harm in trying it.'

'It would be nice to go to the concert. I don't know when we'll get another opportunity to hear Pandit Ravi Shankar,' she said to her mother later. And her father agreed to get the tickets.

The next day as Smita and her father were leaving for the concert, her brother smiled and said, 'Enjoy yourself,' though the words came out in painful gasps. 'Lucky you!'

Sitting besides her father in the gallery, Smita heard as in a dream the thundering welcome the audience gave the great master. Then the first notes came over the air and Smita felt as if the gates of a land of enchantment and wonder were opening. Spellbound, she listened to the unfolding ragas, the slow plaintive notes, the fast twinkling ones, but all the while the plan she had decided on the evening before remained firmly in her mind. 'The chance of a lifetime.' She heard Anant's voice in every beat of the tabla.

The concert came to an end and the audience gave the artistes a standing ovation.

A large moustachioed man made a long boring speech. Then came the presentation of bouquets. Then more applause and the curtain came down. The people began to move towards the exits.

Now was the time. Smita wriggled her way through the crowds towards the stage. Then she went up the steps that led to the wings, her heart beating loudly. In the wings a small crowd had gathered to talk about the evening concert, to help carry bouquets and teacups and instruments.

He was there, standing with the man who played the tabla for him—the great wizard of music, Ustad Allah Rakha. Her knees felt weak, her tongue dry. But she went up, and standing before them, her hands folded, 'Oh Sir,' she burst out.

'Yes?' he asked questioningly but kindly. And her story came pouring out, the story of her brother who lay sick at home and of how he longed to hear him and the Ustad play.

'Will you come to Aunt Sushila's house and play for him?' she asked at the end breathlessly. 'Please,' she begged, 'please come.'

'Little girl,' said the moustachioed man who had made the long speech. 'Panditji is a busy man. You must not bother him with such requests.'

But Pandit Ravi Shankar smiled and motioned him to be quiet. He turned to Ustad Sahib and said, 'What shall we do, Ustad Sahib?'

The Ustad moved the wad of paan from one cheek to another. 'Tomorrow morning we perform for the boy—Yes?' he said.

'Yes,' Panditji replied. 'It's settled then.'

It was a very excited Smita who came home late that night. Anant was awake, breathing the oxygen from the cylinder.

'Did you—did you hear him?' he whispered.

'I did,' she replied, 'and I spoke to him and he'll come tomorrow morning with the tabla Ustad and they'll play for you.'

And the following morning Aunt Sushila's neighbours saw two men get out of a taxi which pulled up outside their block...They could not believe their eyes. 'Is it...It's not possible?' they said.

Pandit Ravi Shankar and Ustad Allah Rakha went up the wooden staircase and knocked softly on the door of Aunt Sushila's apartment. They went in, sat down on the divan by the window and played for the boy, surrounding him with a great and beautiful happiness as life went out of him, gently, very gently.

This is a true story, but all the names except Pandit Ravi Shankar's and Ustad Allah Rakha's have been changed.

Illustrated by Neeta Gangopadhya

·

SORRY, BEST FRIEND!

They had just arrived in Bombay. The schools were still closed, so when Mummy began going to office he stayed at home by himself. Of course Mummy was not happy to leave him alone, but what else could she do? After all, they had come to Bombay so that she could go to office. And he also knew that for a long time after Papa's death Mummy couldn't find any office to go to.

Sonu explained to Mummy, 'Look, I'm not small any more. I'm six. I can look after myself.' But of course that didn't make his fears go away. In Delhi there were always so many people—Dada, Dadi, Chacha, Chachi, all his cousins. And the neighbours.

Mummy always gave all kinds of instructions before leaving. 'Beta, don't open the door except for Bai. And if there is a knock, first find out who it is. Don't lean out of the balcony. Don't turn on the gas. Be sure to have lunch on time.'

But after Mummy left, he felt terribly lonely. He watched TV for a while, or read on the balcony. Then he would look down to see what was happening below on the road. And then eating, and then sleeping! What else was there to do, all alone?

A little after Mummy left, Bai would come. And when her work was finished she too left. Everything was silent next door as well. The people who lived there were away all day.

When Mummy returned in the evening, she would take Sonu for a walk. But she'd be too tired to answer his questions; she would answer one or two and then stop. And although Sonu would still have heaps of questions to ask, he would understand that Mummy was tired and become silent.

One day Bai brought her little girl along. She said to her sternly, 'Stay there and not a word out of you.'

Bai began sweeping and swabbing. The little girl crouched in her corner, silent. She was terribly thin, and not very clean.

'What's your name?'

The little girl just looked frightened.

'Arre! Tell me your name.'

Bai scolded her. 'Didn't you hear, the baba wants to know your name? Tell him at once.'

'Rahiman,' she whispered.

'Do you go to school?'

She shook her head.

'Why not? I'll be going to school soon. A very big one.'

Bai said, 'How can she go to school, Baba? She does all the housework.'

'The housework? But she's still small!'

Sonu wanted to take her to his room and show her his toys and books, but she refused to budge. Finally Sonu brought some of his toys to where she sat. She looked at them then.

When Bai was about to leave, Sonu said quickly, 'Please bring her again tomorrow.'

Bai just smiled and went to the door. But Rahiman turned back to look at Sonu. The door closed and Sonu ran to the balcony to wave bye-bye. Rahiman looked up but didn't wave back.

That evening Sonu had so much to tell Mummy! As Mummy looked at his excited face a thought struck her.

She said something to Bai on Sunday, when she was home, and after that Rahiman came with her mother every day. She no longer crouched silently by the door. Now she would come into his room and look at his toys and books. Sonu would tell her what was in the books or they would play with the toys. When they got tired of that, they made up all kinds of new games. Rahiman began to arrive in clean clothes. Her hair was neatly oiled and plaited. They would eat lunch together. Bai would bring Rahiman in the morning and pick her up in the evening after she had cleaned all the homes in the colony. Now the day flew for Sonu; in the winking of an eye, it seemed, the day was gone.

Sonu and Rahiman would talk to each other for hours. He told her all his secrets, how he was going to be an engine-driver, how his father had been the best in the world, and all about his lovely home in Delhi. Everything. 'Do you know, Mummy, I am Rahiman's best friend,' he told his mother when she came home. 'And when I become an engine-driver I'm going to give her rides all the time.'

The holidays were almost over. On the first of the month, Mummy gave some money to Sonu as she was leaving. 'Keep this carefully. When Bai comes, give it to her. It's her salary.' Then taking out some more rupee notes, 'And this is Rahiman's.'

'Why Rahiman's, Mummy?' Sonu asked.

'Why? Well, doesn't she come here every day to play with you?' smiled Mummy.

What! Did Rahiman play with him because Mummy paid her to? So she wasn't really his best friend? She didn't come because she liked him, but only for money? Sonu felt as if someone had slapped him.

When Rahiman arrived, Sonu said in an unfriendly voice, 'Take it—the money you earned.' But it was Bai who quickly grabbed the money from his hand.

That day Sonu did not speak to Rahiman or play with her. He went with his books to his own corner, and when Rahiman playfully tried to snatch his book away, he flew at her.

'Don't touch it. You can't read or write, stupid!'

Rahiman said nothing. She just gazed at him with all her soul in her eyes. When Mummy came home in the evening Sonu wouldn't speak to her either.

The next day was Sunday, and Mummy had specially asked Rahiman to come on that day. She wanted to take both children to the beach.

Sonu was still angry. He walked ahead of Mummy and Rahiman without saying a word. A cool breeze was blowing, the waves roared in the background and everywhere children were playing in the shiny sand. Some were making sand castles.

'Why don't you make sand castles too,' said Mummy.

Sonu and Rahiman settled down on the sand and each began to make a separate castle. Soon Rahiman's castle was ready. It was beautiful, Sonu had to admit to himself. And strange. It had big and small domes and arches. As for his own castle, even the walls weren't built yet.

'Shabash, Rahiman! It's really lovely,' said Mummy.

Sonu's half-made castle remained unnoticed.

'First she takes our money,' thought Sonu. 'And then Mummy praises her, not me.' His anger boiled over. He got up, ran towards Rahiman's castle and stamped on it.

Rahiman gave a loud sob of surprise. 'He's gone and broken my beautiful house!'

Sonu felt dizzy with anger. He began to jump about on her house as if he had gone mad. 'There, there! There goes your beautiful house. See?'

There was a fight of course. The two children scratched and hit each other. Mummy pulled them apart. After she had calmed them down she took each quietly by the arm and led them home. She tried to get them to make up, but neither Sonu nor Rahiman would listen to her.

That evening Mummy wouldn't talk to Sonu. She didn't give him dinner, and she didn't eat either. The next morning, when Sonu saw that she was in the same mood, he began to mutter, 'First she takes our money. Then you praised her house. And you didn't give me dinner. Now you won't even talk to me!'

He felt he was going to cry any minute. His throat ached with the effort, but somehow he managed not to cry.

As Mummy was leaving for the office, she said, 'I am going to Bai's house to tell her not to bring Rahiman here anymore. You are not her best friend, you are her enemy.'

When he heard Mummy's tone, the tears finally came. Now Mummy asked gently, 'Sonu! Why did you behave so badly? What did Rahiman do to you?'

Sonu sobbed angrily, 'I thought she was my best friend. But she only comes here for money. She doesn't really like to play with me!'

'That's not true.'

'It is. You gave her money.'

'I want you to do something for me, Sonu. Come and see Rahiman's house. I won't go to office. Go and wash your face.'

They went to a cluster of huts at the end of their lane. It was terribly smelly. There was garbage lying around in heaps everywhere. Crows pecked at it, mangy dogs sniffed it, cats chased rats around it. A crowd of thirty or forty women stood around the water tap. Mummy stopped. 'Where is Rahiman's mother?' she asked. Bai emerged from the crowd. 'Where is Rahiman?' asked Mummy.

Soon they were entering a tiny house. It was so dark inside that they could hardly see. Then they saw a small figure at the stove in the smoky corner. It was Rahiman, in torn, filthy clothes. She got up slowly and looked at Sonu. Her eyes were red.

'Rahiman! Sonu has come here to say that he's sorry.'

'No, no, no. Where's the need for that?' Bai quickly broke in. 'Children are always quarrelling and making up.'

'Nobody minds a few fights between friends, Bai!' Mummy said. 'But when people start hating each other...' Then looking at Rahiman she said, 'From

tomorrow Sonu will be going to school. Rahiman too can go now, can't she?'

'Yes, Memsaab. We'll use the money you gave to buy books and get her uniform stitched.'

Sonu turned to Mummy. Mummy was smiling, her eyes on Rahiman's face.

Then Sonu went to Rahiman. He put out his hand and touched her shoulder. And though he whispered, all of them could hear him say, 'Sorry, Best Friend!'

Slightly abridged and translated from the Hindi by Shama Futehally

Illustrated by Damayanti Sharma

Satyajit Ray

·

THE HUNGRY SEPTOPUS

When the doorbell rang again I made an involuntary sound of annoyance. This was the fourth time since the afternoon. How could one do any work? And Kartik too had conveniently disappeared on the pretext of going to the market.

I had to stop writing. When I got up and opened the door, I did not at all expect to see Kanti Babu.

'What a surprise,' I said. 'Come in, come in.'

'Do you recognize me?'

'Well, I nearly didn't.'

I brought him in. Indeed, in these ten years his appearance had changed a lot. Who would now believe that in 1950 this man used to hop around in the forests of Assam with his magnifying glass. He was nearing fifty when I met him there, but he did not have a single grey hair. His zest and energy at that age would have put a young man to shame.

'I notice you have kept up your interest in orchids,' he remarked.

I did have an orchid in a pot on my window, a present Kanti Babu had given me long ago, but it would be wrong to say I had kept up my interest. He had aroused my curiosity about plants. But after he left the country I slowly lost interest in orchids, as I gradually lost interest in most of the other hobbies I had. The only thing that absorbs me now is my writing. Times have changed. It is possible to earn a living by writing and I can almost support my family on the income from my three books now. I still have my job in the office. But I am looking forward to a time when I'll be able to give that up and devote myself entirely to writing, with occasional breaks for travel.

As he sat down Kanti Babu suddenly shivered.

'Are you feeling cold?' I asked. 'Let me close the window. The winter this year in Calcutta...'

'No, no,' he interrupted. 'I get these shivers occasionally. Growing old, you know. It's my nerves.'

There were so many things I wanted to ask him. Kartik had returned, so I told him to make some tea.

'I won't stay long,' Kanti Babu said. 'I happened to see one of your novels. Your publishers gave me your address. I must tell you I've come here with a purpose.'

'Tell me what I can do for you. But tell me...when did you return? Where have you been? Where are you now? There's a lot I want to know.'

'I returned two years ago. I was in America. Now I live in Barasat.'

'Barasat?'

'I have bought a house there.'

'Is there a garden?'

'Yes.'

'And a greenhouse?'

Kanti Babu's earlier house had an excellent greenhouse for his rare plants. What a fantastic collection of unusual plants he had! There were some sixty or sixty-five varieties of orchids alone. One could easily spend a whole day just looking at the flowers.

Kanti Babu paused a little before answering me.

'Yes, there is a greenhouse.'

'That means you are still as interested in plants as you were ten years ago?'

'Yes.'

He was staring at the northern wall of the room. I looked in the same direction: the skin of a Royal Bengal tiger complete with head was hung up there.

'Do you recognize him?' I asked.

'It is the same one, is it not?'

'Yes, see that hole near the ear?'

'You used to be a crack shot. Are you still as good?'

'I don't know. I have not tested myself for some time. I gave up hunting some seven years ago.'

'But why?'

'I had shot enough. I am getting on too, you know. Don't feel like killing animals any more.'

'Have you turned vegetarian?'

'No.'

'Then what is the point? Shooting only means killing. You shoot a tiger, or a crocodile or a buffalo. You get the skin, or stuff the head, or mount the horns to decorate your wall. Some people admire you, some shudder when they look at your trophies. To you they are the reminders of your adventurous youth. But what happens when you eat your goat or your chicken or hilsa? You are not just killing them, but chewing and digesting them as well. Is that in any way better?'

There was nothing I could say in reply. Kartik brought us tea. Kanti Babu was quiet for a while. He shivered once more before picking up the teacup. After a sip he said, 'It is a fundamental law of nature that one creature should eat another and be eaten by a third. Look at that lizard waiting there patiently.'

Just above the calendar of King & Co. a lizard had fixed its unblinking gaze on a moth. We looked at it: at first motionless, it then advanced in slow cautious movements and finally in one swoop it caught the moth.

'Well done,' Kanti Babu commented. 'That will do for his dinner. Food, food is the primary concern in life. Tigers eat men, men eat goats, and goats, what do they not eat? If you begin to reflect on this, it seems so savage and primitive. But this is the law of the universe. There is no escape from it. Creation would come to a standstill if this process were to stop.'

'It might be better to become a vegetarian,' I ventured.

'Who says so? Do you think leaves and vegetables do not have life?'

'Of course they do. Thanks to you and Jagdish Bose I am always aware of that. But it is not the same kind of life, is it? Plants and animals can't be the same.'

'You think they are quite different?'

'Aren't they? Look at their differences. Trees cannot walk, cannot express their feelings, and they have no way of letting us know that they can feel. Don't you agree?'

Kanti Babu looked as if he was about to say something but didn't. He finished his tea and sat quietly with lowered eyes for sometime, then turned his gaze on me. His anxious, haunted stare made me uneasy with the apprehension of some unknown danger. How much his appearance had changed!

Then he began to speak very slowly. 'Parimal, I live twenty-one miles from here. At the age of fifty-eight I have taken the trouble of going all the way to College Street to find your address from your publisher. And now I'm here. I hope you realize that without a special reason I would not have made this effort. Do you? Or have you lost your common sense writing those silly novels? Perhaps you are thinking of me as an interesting "type" you can use in a story.'

I blushed. Kanti Babu was not very wrong. Indeed I was toying with the possibility of using him as a character in one of my novels.

'If you cannot relate your writing to life, Parimal, your books will always remain superficial. And you must not forget that however vivid your imagination, it can never be stranger than truth... Anyway, I have not come here to preach. As a matter of fact, I have come to beg you for a favour.'

I wondered what kind of help he needed from me.

'Do you still have your gun, or have you got rid of it?'

I was a little taken aback at his question. What did he have in mind? I said,

'I still have it, though it must be pretty rusty. Why do you ask?'

'Can you come to my house tomorrow with your gun?'

I looked at his face closely. He did not seem to be joking. 'And cartridges too of course,' he added. I didn't know what to say. Was he perhaps a bit touched in the head, I wondered, although his conversation did not show it? He had always been a bit eccentric, otherwise why should he risk his life in the jungle looking for strange plants?

'I don't mind coming with the gun,' I said, 'but I am very curious to know the reason. Are there wild animals or burglars around where you live?'

'I will tell you everything when you come. You may not finally need the gun, and even if you do, I promise I won't involve you in any act that is punishable by law.'

Kanti Babu rose to go. Putting his hand on my shoulder he said, 'I have come to you, Parimal, because when I

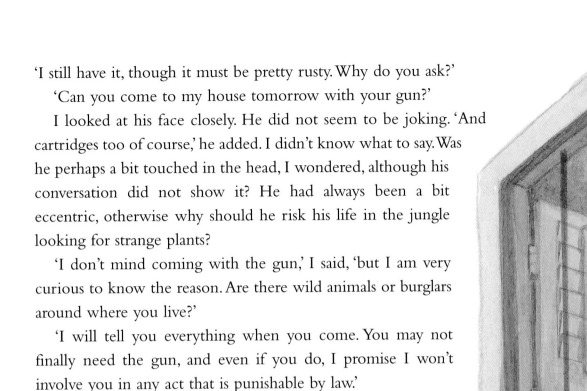

saw you last you like me were attracted to adventure. I have never had much to do with human society, and now my contact is even less. Among my few friends and acquaintances, I can think of no one with your gifts.'

The thrill of adventure which I used to feel in my veins seemed to return momentarily. I said, 'Tell me how to get there, and when, and where...'

'Yes, I'll tell you. Take the Jessore Road straight up to Barasat station, and then you'll have to ask. Anyone will be able to tell you about the Madhumurali lake, about four miles from the station. There is an old indigo planter's bungalow near the lake. Next to that is my house. I hope you have a car?'

'No, but I have a friend who does.'

'Who is this friend?'

'Abhijit. He was with me in college.'

'What sort of person is he? Do I know him?'

'Probably not. But he is a nice chap. I mean he is all right if you are thinking of trustworthiness.'

'Well, bring him along then. Come at any rate. I don't have to tell you that the matter is urgent. Try to reach well before sunset.'

***

We don't have a telephone in the house. I walked to the corner of the road and rang up Abhijit from the Republic Chemists.

'Come right over,' I said. 'I have something very important to tell you.'

'I know. You want me to listen to your new story. I'm afraid I'll fall asleep again.'

'It's not that. Quite a different matter.'

'What is it? Why can't you speak up?'

'There's a mastiff pup going. The man's sitting in my house.'

It was impossible to get Abhijit to stir out unless one used a dog as a bait. In his kennel he had eleven varieties of dogs from five continents, three of them prize winners. Five years ago he was not so crazy about dogs, but now he could think and speak of nothing else.

Other than his love of dogs, Abhijit had one good quality: a total faith in my ability and judgement. When no publisher would agree to take my first novel, Abhijit bore the cost of production. He said, 'I don't understand these things, but you have written it and so it cannot be downright trash. The publishers must be fools.' The book sold rather well and brought me some fame, thus confirming Abhijit's faith in me.

When it turned out that the mastiff story wasn't true, I got what I deserved: one of Abhi's stinging whacks on the shoulder. But I didn't mind because Abhijit agreed to my proposal.

'Let's go. We have not had an outing for a long time. The last one was the snipe shooting out at the Sonarpur swamps. But who is this man? What is the story? Why don't you give me more details?'

'He did not give me any more details. How can I tell you more? But it is better that there should be some mystery. It gives us an opportunity to exercise our imagination.'

'At least tell me who the man is.'

'Kanti Charan Chatterjee. Does the name mean anything to you? At one time he was Professor of Botany at Scottish Church College. Then he left teaching to travel around collecting rare plant specimens. He did a lot of research and published some papers. He had a superb collection of plants—specially orchids.'

'How did you meet him?'

'We were once together in the Kaziranga forest bungalow in Assam. I had gone there hoping to bag a tiger. He was looking for nepenthes.'

'Looking for what?'

'Nepenthes. That's the botanical name. The pitcher plant to you and me. Grows in the forests of Assam. Lives on insects. I have not seen it myself, but this is what Kanti Babu told me.'

'Insect-eater? A plant? Eats insects?'

'I can see you never read botany.'

'No. I didn't.'

'Well you don't have to be sceptical. You can see pictures of these plants in textbooks.'

'Well, go on.'

'There isn't much to say after that. I got my tiger and came back. He stayed on. I was scared that some day he would be bitten by a snake or attacked by a wild animal. We did not meet more than once or twice after returning to Calcutta. But I thought of him often, because for a short time I too got hung up on orchids. He had told me he'd bring some new specimens for me from America.'

'America? So he's been to America?'

'One of his research papers was published in a botanical journal abroad. He became quite well-known because of it and was invited to a conference of botanists. That was way back in fifty-one or two. After that I did not meet him until today.'

'What did he do all these years?'

'I don't yet know. But I hope we will know tomorrow.'

'He's not a crackpot, is he?'

'Not more than you at any rate. You and your dogs are no better than he with his plants.'

We drove along Jessore Road towards Barasat station in Abhijit's Standard. 'We' included, apart from Abhijit and I, a third creature: Abhijit's dog Badshah. This was my mistake. I should have known that unless specifically forbidden Abhijit was sure to bring one of his eleven dogs.

Badshah was a brown Rampur hound. Large and strong, he occupied the whole of the back seat. His face stuck outside the window, he seemed rather appreciative of the wide expanse of green paddy fields. Occasionally, he would snort contemptuously at the village dogs by the roadside.

When I had hinted that Badshah's presence may not be necessary on this trip, Abhijit had retorted, 'I've brought him because I haven't much faith in your gunmanship. You have not touched a rifle for years. If there is danger Badshah will be more useful. His sense of smell is extraordinary and you know how brave he is.'

There was no difficulty in finding Kanti Babu's house. We reached by about two-thirty in the afternoon. After we entered the gate a driveway led to his bungalow. At the back of the house there was a large dried up shirish tree next to a tin shed which looked like a factory. Facing the house, across the road, was the garden, and beyond the garden a longish tin shed in which a number of glittering glass cases stood, arranged in a row.

Kanti Babu welcomed us but frowned a little at Badshah.

'Is this dog trained?' he asked.

Abhi said, 'He obeys me. But if there are untrained dogs around I can't say what he might do. Do you have dogs?'

'No, I don't. But please tie him up here to this window in the sitting-room.'

Abhijit looked at me sideways and winked, but tied the dog up nevertheless like an obedient boy. Badshah registered a mild protest, but seemed to accept the situation.

We sat on cane chairs in the veranda outside. Kanti Babu told us that his servant, Prayag, had injured his right hand, so he himself had made some tea for us and kept it in a flask; we could ask for it when we wanted it.

I could not imagine what untold danger might be lurking in a peaceful place like this. Everything was quiet except for the chirping of birds. I felt very silly carrying the rifle and put it down against the wall.

Abhi is basically a city man who cannot sit still. The beauty of the countryside, the songs of unknown birds—these things don't move him much. He fidgeted for a while and then spoke abruptly, 'I heard from Parimal how you were nearly killed by a tiger in the forests of Assam while looking for some outlandish plant.'

Abhi is fond of making his speech dramatic by exaggerating things. I was afraid he might offend Kanti Babu. But he only smiled and said, 'To you danger in the forest invariably means a tiger, doesn't it? Most people seem to think so. But... No I did not meet a tiger. Once, I was bitten by a leech, but that was nothing.'

'Did you get the plant?'

'Which plant?'

'Pitcher or pewter or whatever plant you call it.'

'Oh, you mean nepenthes. Yes I did. I still have it. I'll show you. Now I have lost interest in most other plants except the carnivorous. I have disposed of most of the orchids too.'

When Kanti Babu went inside, Abhi and I looked at each other. Flesh-eating plants! I vaguely remembered a page from my botany textbook in college, and a few pictures seen fifteen years ago. Kanti Babu returned with a bottle which turned out to be full of grasshoppers, beetles and other insects of assorted size. The stopper of the bottle was pierced with holes like the lid of a pepper pot. 'Feeding time,' he announced. 'Come with me.'

We proceeded to the tin shed which had glass cases under it. Each case contained a plant of a different kind, none of which I had seen before.

'These plants are not to be found in our country,' Kanti Babu said. 'None except the nepenthes. One is from Nepal, another from Africa. The rest have all been brought from Central America.'

Abhijit wanted to know how these plants stayed alive in our soil.

'They have nothing to do with the soil,' Kanti Babu replied.

'How?'

'They do not get nourishment from the soil. Just as human beings get food from outside, and can comfortably survive in most countries besides their own, these too thrive as long as they get the right food, wherever they might be.'

Kanti Babu stopped near one of the glass cases. Inside it was a strange plant with green leaves about two inches long, with serrated white edges like sets of teeth. The glass case had a round door the same size as the mouth of the bottle. With very swift movements Kanti Babu opened this door, uncorked the bottle and pushed the mouth of the bottle through the door. As soon as a moth emerged from the bottle, he quickly withdrew the bottle and shut the door. The moth flitted about for a while and then settled on a leaf. The leaf immediately folded itself in the middle and trapped the moth in a tight grip. The grooves of the teeth fitted into each other so snugly that the moth had no chance of escaping from this cage.

I had never seen a trap designed by nature which was so strange and so frightening.

In a choked voice Abhi asked, 'Is there any certainty that the insect will always sit on the leaf?'

'Of course. These plants emit a smell which attracts insects. This one is called Venus' flytrap, brought from Central America. It is listed in all textbooks of botany,' Kanti Babu said.

I watched the insect with fascination. It had thrashed about a bit at first, but now it looked listless. The pressure of the leaf on it increased. The plant was no less predatory than a lizard.

Abhi tried to force a smile. 'It won't be a bad idea to have a plant like this in the house. Easy way to get rid of vermin. No more sprinkling of DDT powder to kill cockroaches.'

'No, this plant won't do,' Kanti Babu said. 'It won't be able to digest cockroaches. Its leaves are too small.'

Inside the next glass case we saw a plant with long leaves like those of lilies. From the tips of each leaf hung a pouch-shaped thing. I recognized it from the pictures I had seen.

'This is the nepenthes or the pitcher plant,' Kanti Babu explained. 'Its appetite is bigger. When I first got it I found the remains of a small bird inside the pouch.'

'Good heavens!' Abhi shuddered. 'What does it live on now?' His casual attitude was changing to awe.

'Cockroaches, butterflies, caterpillars, things like that. Once, I had caught a mouse in a trap, which I tried to feed to the plant, and the plant did not seem to mind. But overeating can be fatal for them. The plants are very greedy and do not know their natural limit.'

We moved from one glass case to another with mounting fascination. Butterwort, sundew, bladderwort, some of these I recognized from pictures seen earlier, but the rest were totally strange and unbelievable. Kanti Babu had about twenty varieties of carnivorous plants, some of which were not to be found in any collection in the world.

The most exquisite of them was the sundew. It had glistening drops of water surrounding the furry texture of its leaf. Kanti Babu took a tiny piece of meat, about the size of a cardamom seed and tied it to a piece of string. When he gently lowered the string on the leaf, even with the naked eye we could see the hair on the leaf rear up greedily towards the meat.

Kanti Babu withdrew the string and explained that if he had lowered it further, the leaf would have grabbed the meat like the flytrap, and after sqeezing out all the nourishment from it, would have thrown away the rest. 'No different from the way you or I eat—what do you say?'

From the shed we came out into the garden. The shadow of the shirish tree had lengthened on the grass. It was about four in the afternoon.

'Most of these plants have been written about,' Kanti Babu continued, 'but the strangest specimen in my collection will not be listed anywhere unless I write about it. That is the one you must see now. Then you will know why I have asked you to come today. Come Parimal, come Abhijit Babu.'

We followed him towards the shed that looked like a factory. The padlocked metal door was flanked by two windows on either side. Kanti Babu pushed one open and peered in. Then he asked us to come and look. Abhi and I bent over the window.

The western wall of the room had two skylights high up near the ceiling, through whose glass panes some light filtered in to partially illuminate the place. What stood inside the room did not look like a plant at all. It resembled an animal with several thick antennae. Slowly we could distinguish the trunk of the tree rising up to about eight or ten feet. From about a foot below the top of the trunk and around it, sprouted the antennae. I counted seven of them. The trunk was pale and smooth with brown spots all over. The antennae appeared limp and lifeless now, but a shiver ran down my spine as I looked at them. When our eyes got used to the half-light we noticed another thing. The floor of the room was littered with feathers.

I don't know how long we stood transfixed. Finally Kanti Babu spoke, 'The tree is asleep now, but it is almost time for it to wake up.'

Abhi asked in a tone of disbelief, 'It is not really a tree, is it?'

'Since it grows from the ground what else can it be called? Though I must say it does not behave very much like a tree. There is no name for it in the dictionary.'

'What do you call it?'

'Septopus. In Bengali you might call it saptapash, "pash" meaning a coil or a knot, as in "nag-pash".'

As we walked back towards the house I asked him where he had found this specimen.

'In a dense forest near the Nicaragua lake in Central America,' he said.

'Did you have to search very hard?'

'I knew it grew in that region. You may not have heard of Professor Duncan, the explorer and botanist. Well, he lost his life looking for rare plants in Central America. His body was never found and no one knows exactly how he died. This plant was mentioned in the last pages of his diary.

'I took the first opportunity to go to Nicaragua. From Guatemala onwards, I heard the local people talk about this plant, which they called the Satan Tree. Later I found quite a few of them, and actually saw them eating monkeys and armadillos. After a great deal of searching I found a plant small enough to take away with me. Look how much it has grown in two years.'

'What does it eat now?'

'Whatever I give it. I have sometimes caught mice in a trap for it. I told Prayag if he ever finds a dog or a cat run over by a car, he should bring it for the plant. It has digested these too. I have given it whatever meat you and I eat: chicken, goat. But recently its appetite has grown so much that I cannot satisfy its demands any more. When it wakes up at about this time of day, it is very agitated and restless. Yesterday there nearly was a disaster. Prayag had gone inside the room to feed it chicken. It has to be fed the way an elephant is. First a lid opens at the top of the trunk. It takes the food up with one of the antennae and puts it inside the hole on top. Each time it puts some food inside the Septopus is quiet for a while. If after a while the Septopus begins to wave the antennae again, it means it is still hungry.

'Till now two chickens or a small goat a day used to be enough for the Septopus. Since yesterday something seems to have changed. Prayag came away as usual after the second chicken. When he could still hear the sound of thrashing antennae, he went in again to find out what the matter was.

'I was in my room, writing my journal. When I heard a sudden scream I rushed there. A gruesome sight greeted me: one of the Septopus' antennae held Prayag's right hand in a vice-like grip while Prayag pulled with all his strength to set it free. Another antenna was greedily approaching to take hold of him from the other side.

'Without losing any time I hit the antenna very hard with my stick. Then with both hands I pulled Prayag away and just managed to save him. What worries me most is that the Septopus tore off a bit of Prayag's flesh, and with my own eyes I saw it put it inside its mouth.'

We had reached the veranda. Kanti Babu sat down and pulled out a handkerchief to wipe his forehead.

'I had never realized until now that the Septopus is attracted to human flesh. It may be greed or it may be some kind of viciousness, but after what I saw yesterday, I have no alternative but to kill it. Yesterday I tried poisoning its food, but it is too clever for that. It touched the food with the antenna and threw it away. The only way left is to shoot it. Now you know, Parimal, why I have asked you to come.'

I considered this for a while. 'Are you sure a bullet can kill it?' I asked.

'I don't know whether it will die. But I am fairly certain that it has a brain. There is enough evidence that it can think. I have been near it so many times, but it has never attacked me. It knows me just as a dog knows its master. There may be a reason for its being aggressive with Prayag. You see, Prayag sometimes tries to tease the Septopus. He would tempt it with food and then withhold it—or take food very near its antenna and then take it away to see the fun. It does have a brain, and it is located where it should be, that is, in the head—the top part of the trunk around which the antennae have grown. That is the place where you will have to aim your shot.'

Abhijit quickly butted in, 'That is easy. You can find out in a minute. Parimal, take your rifle.'

Kanti Babu raised his hand to stop him. 'Does one shoot while the victim is asleep? Parimal, what does your hunting code say?'

'Killing a sleeping animal is against all codes. Specially when the victim cannot move. It is quite out of the question.'

Kanti Babu brought the flask and served us tea. About fifteen minutes after we had finished drinking it the Septopus woke up.

For some time Badshah had been getting restless in the front room. But now a sudden swish and a whining sound made Abhi and I rush there to see what the matter was. Badshah was frantically trying to break free from the chain. Abhi tried to restrain him by raising his voice. Just then a strange sharp smell filled the air. The smell as well as a loud thrashing sound seemed to be coming from the direction of the tin shed.

It is difficult to describe the smell. I had to undergo surgery once in my childhood to get my tonsils removed. The smell brought back memories of the chloroform they had given me during the operation. Kanti Babu rushed into the room. 'Come, it is time.'

'What is that smell?' I asked.

'The Septopus. This is the smell they emit to attract food...'

Before he could finish, Badshah in one desperate pull managed to jerk open his collar, and pushing Kanti Babu down on the floor, rushed towards the source of the smell.

'Disaster!' Abhi shouted as he ran after the dog.

When I reached the tin shed with my loaded rifle a few seconds later, I saw Badshah disappear through the window in spite of Abhi's attempts to stop him. As Kanti Babu opened the padlocked door we heard the death howl of the Rampur hound. We rushed in to find that one antenna was not enough to hold Badshah. The Septopus was enclosing the dog in a fatal embrace first with one, then with a second and a third antenna.

Kanti Babu yelled at us, 'Don't go a step forward. Parimal, shoot.'

As I was about to take aim Abhijit stopped me. I realized how much his dog meant to him. Heedless of Kanti Babu's warning he advanced towards the Septopus and wrenched free one of the three antennae that held Badshah.

My blood turned to water as I watched this frightening spectacle. All the three antennae closed in on Abhi now, letting go of the dog, while the other four slowly swayed forward like greedy tongues tempted at the prospect of human blood.

Kanti Babu urged, 'Shoot, Parimal, shoot. There, at the head.'

I fixed my eyes on the Septopus and watched a lid slowly open on the top of the trunk revealing a hole. The antennae were carrying Abhi towards that hole. Abhi's face was white and his eyes bulged.

In a moment of extreme crisis—I have noticed this before also—my nerves become calm and controlled as if by magic.

With steady hands I held my rifle and with unerring aim shot at the point between two round spots on the head of the Septopus.

I remember, too, the blood that spurted out like a fountain. I think I saw the antennae suddenly going limp, releasing their grip on Abhi. And then the smell grew and enveloped my consciousness.

* * *

It has been four months since that incident. I have at last been able to resume work on my incomplete novel.

Badshah could not be saved. Abhi has acquired a mastiff pup and a Tibetan dog in the meanwhile, and is looking for another Rampur hound. Two of Abhi's ribs had been fractured. After being in plaster for two months, he is on his feet again.

Kanti Babu came yesterday. He said he was thinking of getting rid of all his carnivorous plants. 'I think I'll do some research on common domestic vegetables like gourd, beans and brinjal. You have done so much for me. If you want I'll give you some of my plants. The nepenthes for example. At least your house will be free of insects.'

'No, thank you,' I said. 'Throw them all out if you want to. I don't need a plant to rid my house of insects.'

'Ditto, ditto,' said the lizard from behind the calendar of King & Co.

Translated from the Bengali by Meenakshi Mukherjee

Illustrated by Suddhasattwa Basu

Salman Rushdie

—————— ■ ——————

FROM **HAROUN AND THE SEA OF STORIES**

There was once, in the country of Alifbay, a sad city, the saddest of cities, a city so ruinously sad that it had forgotten its name. It stood by a mournful sea full of glumfish, which were so miserable to eat that they made people belch with melancholy even though the skies were blue.

In the north of the sad city stood mighty factories in which (so I'm told) sadness was actually manufactured, packaged and sent all over the world, which never seemed to get enough of it. Black smoke poured out of the chimneys of the sadness factories and hung over the city like bad news.

And in the depths of the city, beyond an old zone of ruined buildings that looked like broken hearts, there lived a happy young fellow by the name of Haroun, the only child of the storyteller Rashid Khalifa, whose cheerfulness was famous throughout that unhappy metropolis, and whose never-ending stream of tall, short and winding tales had earned him not one but two nicknames. To his admirers he was Rashid the Ocean of Notions, as stuffed with cheery stories as the sea was full of glumfish; but to his jealous rivals he was the Shah of Blah. To his wife, Soraya, Rashid was for many years as loving a husband as anyone could wish for, and during these years Haroun grew up in a home in which, instead of misery and frowns, he had his father's ready laughter and his mother's sweet voice raised in song.

Then something went wrong. (Maybe the sadness of the city finally crept in through their windows.)

The day Soraya stopped singing, in the middle of a line, as if someone had thrown a switch, Haroun guessed there was trouble brewing. But he never suspected how much.

* * *

Rashid Khalifa was so busy making up and telling stories that he didn't notice that Soraya no longer sang; which probably made things worse. But then Rashid was a busy man, in constant demand, he was the Ocean of Notions, the famous Shah of Blah. And what with all his rehearsals and performances, Rashid was so often on stage that he lost track of what was going on in his own home. He sped around the city and the country telling stories, while Soraya stayed home, turning cloudy and even a little thunderous and brewing up quite a storm.

Haroun went with his father whenever he could, because the man was a magician, it couldn't be denied. He would climb up on to some little makeshift stage in a dead-end alley packed with raggedy children and toothless old-timers, all squatting in the dust; and once he got going even the city's many wandering cows would stop and cock their ears, and monkeys would jabber approvingly from rooftops and the parrots in the trees would imitate his voice.

Haroun often thought of his father as a Juggler, because his stories were really lots of different tales juggled together, and Rashid kept them going in a sort of dizzy whirl, and never made a mistake.

Where did all these stories come from? It seemed that all Rashid had to do was to part his lips in a plump red smile and out would pop some brand-new saga, complete with sorcery, love-interest, princesses, wicked uncles, fat aunts, moustachioed gangsters in yellow check pants, fantastic locations, cowards, heroes, fights, and half a dozen catchy, hummable tunes. 'Everything comes from somewhere,' Haroun reasoned, 'so these stories can't simply come out of thin air...?'

But whenever he asked his father this most important of questions, the Shah of Blah would narrow his (to tell the truth) slightly bulging eyes, and

pat his wobbly stomach, and stick his thumb between his lips while he made ridiculous drinking noises, *glug glug glug*. Haroun hated it when his father acted this way. 'No, come on, where do they come from really?' he'd insist, and Rashid would wiggle his eyebrows mysteriously and make witchy fingers in the air.

'From the great Story Sea,' he'd reply. 'I drink the warm Story Waters and then I feel full of steam.'

Haroun found this statement intensely irritating. 'Where do you keep this hot water, then?' he argued craftily. 'In hot-water bottles, I suppose. Well, I've never seen any.'

'It comes out of an invisible Tap installed by one of the Water Genies,' said Rashid with a straight face. 'You have to be a subscriber.'

'And how do you become a subscriber?'

'Oh,' said the Shah of Blah, 'that's much Too Complicated To Explain.'

'Anyhow,' said Haroun grumpily, 'I've never seen a Water Genie, either.' Rashid shrugged. 'You're never up in time to see the milkman,' he pointed out, 'but you don't mind drinking the milk. So now kindly desist from this Iffing and Butting and be happy with the stories you enjoy.' And that was the end of that.

Except that one day Haroun asked one question too many, and then all hell broke loose.

* * *

The Khalifas lived in the downstairs part of a small concrete house with pink walls, lime-green windows and blue-painted balconies with squiggly metal railings, all of which made it look (in Haroun's view) more like a cake than a building. It wasn't a grand house, nothing like the skyscrapers where the super-rich folks lived; then again, it was nothing like the dwellings of the poor, either. The poor lived in tumbledown shacks made of old cardboard boxes and plastic sheeting, and these shacks were glued together by despair. And then there were the super-poor, who had no homes at all. They slept on pavements and in the doorways of shops, and had to pay rent to local gangsters for doing even that. So the truth is that Haroun was lucky; but luck has a way of running out without the slightest warning. One minute you've got a lucky star watching over you and the next instant it's done a bunk.

***

In the sad city, people mostly had big families; but the poor children got sick and starved, while the rich kids overate and quarrelled over their parents' money. Still Haroun wanted to know why his parents hadn't had more children, but the only answer he ever got from Rashid was no answer at all.

'There's more to you, young Haroun Khalifa, than meets the blinking eye.'

Well, what was *that* supposed to mean? 'We used up our full quota of child-stuff just in making you,' Rashid explained. 'It's all packed in there, enough for maybe four-five kiddies. Yes, sir, more to you than the blinking eye can see.'

Straight answers were beyond the powers of Rashid Khalifa, who would never take a short cut if there was a longer, twistier road available. Soraya gave Haroun a simpler reply. 'We tried,' she sadly said. 'This child business is not such an easy thing. Think of the poor Senguptas.'

The Senguptas lived upstairs. Mr Sengupta was a clerk at the offices of the City Corporation and he was as sticky-thin and whiny-voiced and mingy as his wife Oneeta was generous and loud and wobbly-fat. They had no children at all, and as a result Oneeta Sengupta paid more attention to Haroun than he really cared for. She brought him sweetmeats (which was fine), and ruffled his hair (which wasn't), and when she hugged him the great cascades of her flesh seemed to surround him completely, to his considerable alarm.

Mr Sengupta ignored Haroun, but was always talking to Soraya, which Haroun didn't particularly like, particularly as the fellow would launch into criticisms of Rashid the storyteller whenever he thought Haroun wasn't listening. 'That husband of yours, excuse me if I mention,' he would start in his thin whiny voice. 'He's got his head stuck in the air and his feet off the ground. What are all these stories? Life is not a storybook or a joke shop. All this fun will come to no good. What's the use of stories that aren't even true?'

Haroun, listening hard outside the window, decided he did not care for Mr Sengupta, this man who hated stories and storytellers: he didn't care for him one little bit.

What's the use of stories that aren't even true? Haroun couldn't get the terrible question out of his head. However, there were people who thought Rashid's stories were useful. In those days it was almost election time, and the Grand Panjandrums of various political parties all came to Rashid smiling their fat-cat smiles, to beg him to tell his stories at their rallies and nobody else's. It was well known that if you could get Rashid's magic tongue on your side then your troubles were over. Nobody ever believed anything a politico said, even though they pretended as hard as they could that they were telling the truth. (In fact, this was how everyone knew they were lying.) But everyone had complete faith in Rashid, because he always admitted that everything he told them was completely untrue and made up out of his own head. So the politicos needed Rashid to help them win the people's votes. They lined up

outside his door with their shiny faces and fake smiles and bags of hard cash. Rashid could pick and choose.

∗ ∗ ∗

On the day that everything went wrong, Haroun was on his way home from school when he was caught in the first downpour of the rainy season.

Now, when the rains came to the sad city, life became a little easier to bear. There were delicious pomfret in the sea at that time of the year, so people could have a break from the glumfish; and the air was cool and clean, because the rain washed away most of the black smoke billowing out of the sadness factories. Haroun Khalifa loved the feeling of getting soaked to the skin in the first rain of the year, so he skipped about and got a wonderful warm drenching, and opened his mouth to let raindrops plop on to his tongue. He arrived home looking as wet and shiny as a pomfret in the sea.

Miss Oneeta was standing on her upstairs balcony, shaking like a jelly; and if it hadn't been raining, Haroun might have noticed that she was crying. He went indoors and found Rashid the storyteller looking as if he'd stuck his face out of the window, because his eyes and cheeks were soaking wet, even though his clothes were dry.

Haroun's mother, Soraya, had run off with Mr Sengupta.

At eleven a.m. precisely, she had sent Rashid into Haroun's room, telling him to search for some missing socks. A few seconds later, while he was busy with the hunt (Haroun was good at losing socks), Rashid heard the front door slam, and, an instant later, the sound of a car in the lane. He returned to the living room to find his wife gone and a taxi speeding away around the corner. 'She must have planned it all very carefully,' he thought. The clock still stood at eleven o'clock exactly. Rashid picked up a hammer and smashed the clock to bits. Then he broke every other clock in the house, including the one on Haroun's bedside table.

The first thing Haroun said on hearing the news of his mother's departure was, 'What did you have to break my clock for?'

Soraya had left a note full of all the nasty things Mr Sengupta used to say about Rashid: 'You are only interested in pleasure, but a proper man would know that life is a serious business. Your brain is full of make-believe, so there is no room in it for facts. Mr Sengupta has no imagination at all. This is okay by me.' There was a postscript. 'Tell Haroun I love him, but I can't help it, I have to do this now.'

Rainwater dripped on to the note from Haroun's hair. 'What to do, son,' Rashid pleaded piteously. 'Storytelling is the only work I know.'

When he heard his father sounding so pathetic, Haroun lost his temper and shouted: 'What's the point of it? *What's the use of stories that aren't even true?*'

Rashid hid his face in his hands and wept.

Haroun wanted to get those words back, to pull them out of his father's ears and shove them back into his own mouth; but of course he couldn't do that. And that was why he blamed himself when, soon afterwards and in the most embarrassing circumstances imaginable, an Unthinkable Thing happened:

Rashid Khalifa, the legendary Ocean of Notions, the fabled Shah of Blah, stood up in front of a huge audience, opened his mouth, and found that he had run out of stories to tell.

* * *

Haroun is deeply disturbed by his mother's departure. His father, Rashid, is invited to perform by some politicians in the Town of G and the beautiful Valley of K. However, when Rashid the superlative storyteller gets on the stage at a rally in the Town of G, no story comes out of his mouth. He has lost his Gift of the Gab. Rashid reassures his angry paymasters that he will be back in form in the Valley of K.

Haroun is very upset, blames himself and vows to put things right. Haroun and Rashid set off for the Valley of K.

The two shouting men shoved Rashid and Haroun into the back seat of a beaten-up car with torn scarlet seats, and even though the car's cheap radio was playing movie music at top volume, the shouting men went on shouting about the unreliability of storytellers all the way to the rusting iron gates of the Bus Depot. Here Haroun and Rashid were dumped out of the car without ceremony or farewell.

'Expenses of the journey?' Rashid hopefully inquired, but the shouting men shouted, 'More cash demands! Cheek! Cheek of the chappie!' and drove away at high speed, forcing dogs and cows and women with baskets of fruit on their heads to dive out of the way. Loud music and rude words continued to pour out of the car as it zigzagged away into the distance.

Rashid didn't even bother to shake his fist. Haroun followed him towards the Ticket Office across a dusty courtyard with walls covered in strange warnings:

IF YOU TRY TO RUSH OR ZOOM
YOU ARE SURE TO MEET YOUR DOOM

was one of them, and

ALL THE DANGEROUS OVERTAKERS
END UP SAFE AT UNDERTAKERS'

was another, and also

LOOK OUT! SLOW DOWN! DON'T BE FUNNY!
LIFE IS PRECIOUS! CARS COST MONEY!

'There should be one about not shouting at the passengers in the back seat,' Haroun muttered. Rashid went to buy a ticket.

There was a wrestling match at the ticket window instead of a queue, because everyone wanted to be first; and as most people were carrying chickens or children or other bulky items, the result was a free-for-all out of which feathers and toys and dislodged hats kept flying. And from time to time some dizzy fellow with ripped clothes would burst out of the mêlée, triumphantly waving a little scrap of paper: his ticket! Rashid, taking a deep breath, dived into the scrum.

Meanwhile, in the courtyard of the buses, small dust-clouds were rushing back and forth like little desert whirlwinds. Haroun realized that these clouds were full of human beings. There were simply too many passengers at the Bus Depot to fit into the available buses, and, anyhow, nobody knew which bus was leaving first; which made it possible for the drivers to play a mischievous game. One driver would start his engine, adjust his mirrors, and behave as if he were about to leave. At once a bunch of passengers would gather up their suitcases and bedrolls and parrots and transistor radios and rush towards him. Then he'd switch off his engine with an innocent smile; while on the far side of the courtyard, a different bus would start up, and the passengers would start running all over again.

'It's not fair,' Haroun said aloud.

'Correct,' a booming voice behind him answered, 'but but but you'll admit it's too much fun to watch.'

The owner of this voice turned out to be an enormous fellow with a great quiff of hair standing straight up on his head, like a parrot's crest. His face, too, was extremely hairy; and the thought popped into Haroun's mind that all this hair was, well, somehow *feather-like*. 'Ridiculous idea,' he told himself. 'What on earth made me think of a thing like that? It's just plain nonsense, as anyone can see.'

Just then two separate dust-clouds of scurrying passengers collided in an explosion of umbrellas and milk-churns and rope sandals, and Haroun, without meaning to, began to laugh. 'You're a tip-top type,' boomed the fellow with the feathery hair. 'You see the funny side! An accident is truly a sad and cruel thing, but but but—crash! Wham! Spatoosh!—how it makes one giggle and hoot.' Here the giant stood and bowed. 'At your service,' he said. 'My goodname is Butt, driver of the Number One Super Express Mail Coach to the Valley of K.' Haroun thought he should bow, too. 'And my, as you say, goodname is Haroun.'

Then he had an idea, and added: 'If you mean what you say about being at my service, then in fact there is something you can do.'

'It was a figure of speech,' Mr Butt replied. 'But but but I will stand by it!

A figure of speech is a shifty
thing; it can be twisted or it can be
straight. But Butt's a straight man, not a
twister. What's your wish, my young mister?'

Rashid had often told Haroun about the
beauty of the road from the Town of G to the
Valley of K, a road that climbed like a serpent
through the Pass of H towards the Tunnel of I (which
was also known as J). There was snow by the roadside, and
there were fabulous multicoloured birds gliding in the gorges;
and when the road emerged from the Tunnel (Rashid had said),
then the traveller saw before him the most spectacular view on earth,
a vista of the Valley of K with its golden fields and silver mountains and
with the Dull Lake at its heart—a view spread out like a magic carpet,
waiting for someone to come and take a ride. 'No man can be sad who looks
upon that sight,' Rashid had said, 'but a blind man's blindness must feel twice
as wretched then.' So what Haroun asked Mr Butt for was

this: front-row seats in the Mail Coach all the way to the Dull Lake; and a guarantee that the Mail Coach would pass through the Tunnel of I (also known as J) before sunset, because otherwise the whole point would be lost.

'But but but,' Mr Butt protested, 'the hour is already late...' Then, seeing Haroun's face begin to fall, he grinned broadly and clapped his hands. 'But but but so what?' he shouted. 'The beautiful view! To cheer up the sad dad! Before sunset! *No problem.*'

So when Rashid staggered out of the Ticket Office he found Haroun waiting on the steps of the Mail Coach, with the best seats reserved inside, and the motor running.

The other passengers, who were out of breath from their running, and who were covered in dust which their sweat was turning to mud, stared at Haroun with a mixture of jealousy and awe. Rashid was impressed, too. 'As I may have mentioned, young Haroun Khalifa: more to you than meets the blinking eye.'

'Yahoo!' yelled Mr Butt, who was as excitable as any mail service employee. 'Varoom!' he added, and jammed the accelerator pedal right down against the floor.

The Mail Coach rocketed through the gates of the Bus Depot, narrowly missing a wall on which Haroun read this:

IF FROM SPEED YOU GET YOUR THRILL
TAKE PRECAUTION—MAKE YOUR WILL

Excerpts from the chapters, 'The Shah of Blah' and 'The Mail Coach'

Illustrated by Sujasha Dasgupta

Bhisham Sahni

•

THE BOY WITH A CATAPULT

 Our class at school had an odd assortment of boys. There was Harbans Lal who, when asked a difficult question, would take a sip out of his inkpot because he believed it sharpened his wits. If the teacher boxed his ears he would yell, 'Help! Murder!' so loudly that teachers and boys from other classes would come running to see what had happened. This caused much embarrassment to the teacher. If the teacher tried to cane him, he would put his arms round him and implore, 'Forgive me, Your Majesty! You are like Akbar the Great. You are Emperor Ashoka. You are my father, my grandfather, my great grandfather.'

This made the boys giggle and put the teacher out of countenance. This Harbans Lal would catch frogs and tell us, 'If you smear your hands with frog fat you will not feel the teacher's cane.'

But the oddest fellow in the class was Bodh Raj. We were all afraid of him. If he pinched anyone's arm, the arm would swell up as if from a snake-bite. He was utterly callous. He would catch a wasp with his bare fingers, pull out its sting, tie a thread round it and fly it like a kite. He would pounce on a butterfly sitting on a flower and crush it between his fingers; or else stick a pin through it and put it in his notebook.

It was said that if a scorpion stung Bodh Raj the scorpion would fall dead; Bodh Raj's blood was believed to be so full of venom that even snake-bite had no effect on him. He always had a catapult in his hand and was an excellent shot. His favourite targets were birds. He would stand under a tree, take aim and the next moment bird cries would rend the air and the fluff of feathers float down. Or else he would climb up a tree, take away the eggs and completely destroy the nest.

He was vindictive and took pleasure in hurting others. All the boys were scared of him. If Bodh Raj quarrelled with anyone, he would charge at him head-on like a bull, or viciously kick and bite him. Even his mother called him a rakshasa—demon. His pockets bulged with strange things—a live parrot, an assortment of eggs, or a prickly hedgehog.

* * *

My father was given a promotion in his job and we moved into a large bungalow. It was an old-style bungalow on the outskirts of the city. It had brick floors, high walls, a slanting roof and a garden full of trees and shrubs. Though comfortable it seemed rather empty and big, and being far from the city my friends seldom came to visit me.

The only exception was Bodh Raj. He found it good hunting ground. The trees had many nests, monkeys roamed about, and under the bushes lived a pair of mongooses. Behind the house there was a big room, where my mother stored our extra luggage. This room had become a haunt of pigeons. You could hear their cooing all day. Near the broken glass of the ventilator there was also a myna's nest. The floor of the room was littered with feathers, bird droppings, broken eggs, and bits of straw from the nests.

Once, Bodh Raj brought a hedgehog with him. The sight of the black mouth and sharp bristles gave me quite a turn. My mother did not approve of my friendship with Bodh Raj, but she realized that I was lonely and needed company. My mother called him a devil and often told him not to torment birds.

One day my mother said to me, 'If your friend is so fond of destroying nests tell him to clean our storeroom. The birds have made it very filthy.'

I protested, 'You said it's cruel to destroy nests.'

'I didn't suggest he should kill the birds. He can remove the nests without harming them.'

The next time Bodh Raj came I took him to the godown. It was dark and smelly as though we had entered an animal's lair.

I confess I was somewhat apprehensive. What if Bodh Raj acted true to form and destroyed the nests, pulled out the birds' feathers and broke their eggs? I couldn't understand why my mother who discouraged our friendship should have asked me to get Bodh Raj to clear the godown.

Bodh Raj had brought his catapult. He carefully studied the position of the nests under the roof. The two sides of the roof sloped downward with a long supporting beam across. At one end of the beam, near the ventilator, was a myna's nest. I could see bits of cottonwool and rag hanging out. Some pigeons strutted up and down the beam cooing to one another.

'The myna's little ones are up there,' said Bodh Raj aiming with his catapult.

I noticed two tiny yellow beaks peeping out of the nest.

'Look!' Bodh Raj exclaimed, 'This is a Ganga myna. It isn't usually found in these areas. The parents must have got separated from their flock and come here.'

'Where are the parents?' I asked.

'Must have gone in search of food. They should be back soon.' Bodh Raj raised his catapult.

I wanted to stop him but before I could open my mouth there was a whizzing sound, and then a loud clang as the pebble hit the corrugated iron-sheet on the roof.

The tiny beaks vanished. The cooing and tittering ceased. It seemed as if all the birds had been frightened into silence.

Bodh Raj let fly another pebble. This time it struck the rafter. Bodh Raj was proud of his aim; he had missed his target twice and was very angry with himself. When the chicks peeped over the rim of the nest, Bodh Raj had a third try. This time the pebble hit the side of the nest— a few straws and bits of cottonwool fell—but the nest was not dislodged.

Bodh Raj lifted his catapult again. Suddenly a large shadow flitted across the room, blocking the light from the ventilator. Startled we looked up. Gazing down at us menacingly was a large kite with its wings outstretched.

'This must be the kite's nest,' I said.

'No, how can a kite have its nest here? A kite always makes its nest in a tree. This is a myna's nest.'

The chicks began fluttering their wings and shrieking loudly. We held our breath. What would the kite do?

The kite left the ventilator and perched on the rafter. It had folded back its wings. It shook its scraggy neck, and peered to the right, and the left.

The birds' frightened cries filled the air.

'The kite has been coming here every day,' said Bodh Raj.

I realized why broken wings, straw and bits of bird flesh littered the floor. The kite must have ravaged the nest often.

Bodh Raj had not taken his eyes off the kite which was slowly edging its way towards the nest. The cries rose to a crescendo.

I was a bundle of nerves. What difference did it make whether the kite or Bodh Raj killed the myna's young? If the kite had not come Bodh Raj would certainly have made short work of the nest.

Bodh Raj raised his catapult and aimed at the kite.

'Don't hit the kite. It will attack you,' I shouted. But Bodh Raj paid no attention. The pebble missed the kite and hit the ceiling. The kite spread its wings wide and peered down.

'Let's get out of here,' I said, frightened.

'The kite will eat up the little ones.' This sounded rather strange coming from him.

Bodh Raj aimed again. The kite left the rafter and spreading its wings, flew in a semicircle and alighted on the beam. The chicks continued to scream.

Bodh Raj handed me the catapult and some pebbles from his pocket.

'Aim at the kite. Go on hitting it. Don't let it sit down,' he instructed. Then he ran and pulled up a table standing against the wall to the middle of the room.

I didn't know how to use the catapult. I tried once, but the kite had left the beam and flown to another.

Bodh Raj brought the table right under the myna's nest. Then he picked up a broken chair and placed it on the table. He climbed on the chair, gently lifted the nest and slowly stepped down.

'Let's get out of here,' he said, and ran towards the door. I followed.

We went into the garage. It had only one door and a small window in the back wall. A beam ran across its width.

'The kite can't get in here,' he said, and climbing on to a box, placed the nest on the beam.

The myna's young had quietened down. Standing on the box Bodh Raj had his first peep into the nest. I thought that he would pick them both up and put them in his pocket, as he usually did. But after looking at them for a long time he said, 'Bring some water, the chicks are thirsty. We'll put it, drop by drop, into their mouths.'

I brought a glass of water. Both the chicks, beaks open, were panting. Bodh Raj fed them with drops of water. He told me not to touch them, nor did he touch them himself.

'How will their parents know they are here?' I asked.

'They will look for them.'

We stayed in the garage for a long time. Bodh Raj discussed plans to close the ventilator, so that the kite would not be able to enter the godown again. That evening he talked of nothing else.

When Bodh Raj came the next day, he had neither catapult nor pebbles. He carried a bag of seeds. We fed the myna's young and spent hours watching their antics.

Translated from the Hindi by Bhisham Sahni

Illustrated by Sujata Singh

Subhadra Sen Gupta

·

DAL DELIGHT

Sadiq was sitting in his father's food stall, in a small gali in Lucknow, brushing off flies from a platter of biryani, when he saw a man in a silk achkan get off a horse, at their door. Two servants followed the man.

'Looks rich. Is he coming here?' Sadiq wondered.

Sadiq's father Mohammad Qadir looked up from the kebabs he was frying on a huge angeethi, as one of the servants came up and announced, 'Nawab Hasan Ali has arrived.'

The man in silk entered and looked around their small shop. 'I hear you are a famous cook, Mohammad Qadir,' he said in a bored voice. 'I like tasting new dishes. What do you make best?'

'Dal,' said Sadiq's father and went on frying the kebabs.

'Dal? Just dal?' the Nawab asked, surprised.

'I can make biryani and korma and all the usual dishes but you asked me what I make best,' Qadir said calmly.

'But dal! That doesn't sound very exciting. My friends were praising your cooking so much, I expected some new extraordinary dish.'

'But you haven't tasted the dal I make.'

'Fine, I'll taste it. What kind of dal do you make?'

'Urad.'

'Give me some. Let's see what's so special about it.'

'I haven't got any ready now.'

'What!' the Nawab said angrily.

'I make my dal shahi urad only on order,' Qadir said. 'I use a special masala. It takes a day to make. If your honour wishes, I'll prepare it for tomorrow's lunch.'

Nawab Hasan Ali agreed reluctantly. 'I live nearby. You can bring it to my house tomorrow.'

'I'm sorry sir, that's not possible,' said Qadir. Sadiq sighed to himself. His father was being difficult as usual. His Abbajan lost a lot of customers because he was such a fussy cook. And this nawab looked rich.

Nawab Hasan Ali had never met such a rude cook but he was also amused. 'What's the problem now, Qadir mia?'

'Huzoor, to enjoy my dal you will have to come to my shop. It has to be eaten immediately. So your honour, once I call, you will have to come at once.'

'Really? What if I'm late?'

'I'll throw the dal away or give it to the poor,' Qadir replied, sliding some kebabs into the hot oil with a hiss.

Nawab Hasan Ali shook his head. This Qadir was like no cook he had met. 'Ah well,' he thought, 'let's taste his dal, maybe it will be worth the trouble.

'Call me tomorrow when you're ready,' he said and left the stall.

Sadiq sighed with relief. He had been worried that the Nawab would lose his temper and leave. Sadiq knew that nawabs often gave generous rewards to cooks if they liked a dish. His Abbu had nearly spoilt everything. Sadiq was rather scared of his father. When Mohammad Qadir became angry, the neighbours said, crows flew away cawing and street dogs hid behind trees. It was lucky that the Nawab had been in a good mood and agreed to all Qadir's conditions. His father was capable of refusing to cook for the badshah himself if he wasn't treated well.

In the evening Sadiq went with his father to the market to buy the ingredients for the dal shahi urad. Only the best would do, of course. Each grain of urad had to be perfect, no broken bits. Cinnamon sticks, cardamom, coriander, cumin, cloves, garlic pods, onions, ginger and turmeric of the highest quality. Saffron and milk for the fragrant pure ghee. Green, crisp mint leaves for the chutney.

'Aadaab, Qadir mia!' one of the servants who had accompanied Nawab Hasan Ali greeted them at the vegetable shop. 'How's the shopping going for the dal shahi urad?'

'Aadaab,' said Qadir shortly. He didn't like talking unnecessarily.

Sadiq smiled at the man. 'Your Nawabsaab seems to like eating,' he said.

'Ah! Doesn't he!' The man laughed. 'It's his greatest hobby. He is always on the lookout for new food stalls and if he likes a particular preparation he gives fabulous rewards.'

'Really?' Sadiq asked excited. 'What has he given?'

'Well, once he was so pleased by a pasanda and pulao in Aminabad he bought the cook a new shop.'

'A whole shop!' Sadiq exclaimed wide-eyed.

'The Nawab is very rich. Last month he gave a diamond ring to a chef for his phirni.'

Qadir was calling him, so Sadiq had to leave but on the way home he dreamt of the reward his father could get. He knew that his father's dal shahi urad was as good as any pulao or pasanda any cook could prepare.

Early next morning Sadiq set to work with his father. He helped him clean the dal, make ghee, grind turmeric, peel and chop the onions, garlic and ginger. Then he watched Qadir cook the dal. With the dal, Qadir made a light cucumber raita, mint chutney, a vegetable dish of cauliflower and potatoes, a plate of creamy and soft kakori kebabs. And, once the Nawab sat down to eat, he would serve freshly baked tandoori rotis. For dessert there were bowls of phirni. Sadiq had sneaked a quick taste of the dal when his father wasn't looking. It tasted utterly delicious. It was the secret masala that made all the difference.

Everything was ready: the dal in the handi was bubbling gently on the angeethi; balls of dough moist and ready to be slapped into rotis; the raita cooling in an earthen bowl. Qadir turned to his son. 'Go call the Nawab, beta. I'm ready to serve lunch.'

Sadiq ran all the way to Nawab Hasan Ali's haveli. He reached the house panting. 'I've come to call Nawabsaab for lunch. The dal is ready,' he said to the servant.

'Go up to the roof. Nawabsaab is flying kites there.'

Sadiq tore up the stairs to the roof. The Nawab and his friends were completely engrossed in flying kites. Sadiq went up to Hasan Ali and said timidly, 'Nawabsaab, the dal is ready. My father is calling you.'

Hasan Ali looked down at Sadiq. 'Who?' Then he seemed to remember. 'Ah yes, the dal.'

One of his friends laughed. 'Forget the dal, Hasan. Your kite is in danger. The green kite is about to cut it.'

Hasan Ali hurriedly pulled at his kite. 'Just you wait, green kite! I'll get you!' he shouted.

'Nawabsaab...' Sadiq interrupted, worried about his father's temper. 'The food is waiting.'

'Yes, yes,' Hasan Ali said, irritated. 'Tell your father to wait. Can't you see my kite is in danger?'

'Run along, boy,' one of his friends said impatiently. 'Can't you see Nawabsaab is busy?'

'But the dal...' Sadiq gave up and sadly walked away. All his dreams were fading away. He knew what would happen. He knew his Abbu's temper. The moment Qadir heard that the Nawab preferred to fly kites to tasting his dal, he would fly into a rage and give the handi of dal to the first beggar. They could forget about the reward. Sadiq felt like crying.

On reaching home he looked up. The Nawab's kite was flying overhead. And his friend Aman was flying a kite from his rooftop across the lane. Suddenly a wonderful idea struck Sadiq. He ran to Aman's rooftop. 'Aman, do me a favour! See that blue-and-silver kite? Cut it. Fast!'

'Sure. No problem,' said Aman grinning. He was a champion kite flier. He made a special kite string with a layer of ground glass that could cut through anything.

Sadiq raced back to the Nawab's house. He ran up the stairs and reached the roof just as Aman had positioned his kite directly above the Nawab's. Aman gave a sharp tug. 'Oh no!' Hasan Ali groaned in dismay as his kite was cut and wafted down towards the ground.

'Huzoor...' Sadiq said, 'the food is waiting. The dal is delicious.'

'Oh yes, yes.' The Nawab suddenly remembered the special dal.

'Now the kite's gone, let's go and eat.'

Sadiq raced ahead, his heart thumping nervously. 'Oh Allah,' he prayed, 'don't let Abbu lose his temper. Please, don't let it be too late.'

The Nawab and his friends entered the stall. The best room had been readied for them. As they sat down on the carpet, Qadir came in with the dal and Sadiq followed with piping hot rotis dripping with butter.

Sadiq held his breath as Nawab Hasan Ali broke a piece of roti, dipped it in the dal shahi urad, put it in his mouth, chewed slowly and then closed his eyes. 'Ah!' he said softly. Sadiq let go of his breath.

The Nawab dipped a second piece of roti in the dal, scooped some raita with it, savoured it and said, 'Wah! Qadir mia, your dal shahi urad is truly heavenly! I have never tasted anything better. Even a roganjosh pales before it.' After a few more mouthfuls, Hasan Ali continued, 'You deserve a reward. Tell me what would you like?'

For the first time that day Mohammad Qadir smiled. 'I would like to have a bigger food stall, huzoor. Near the Imambara.'

'Done!' said Hasan Ali, dipping into the vegetable and helping himself to a kakori kebab. He called one of his servants. The servant bowed and put a bag full of money in Qadir's hand. 'This should be enough for your new shop,' said Nawab Hasan Ali. 'Now give me some more of your dal shahi urad and a roti.'

Watching his father serve the Nawab and his guests Sadiq grinned to himself. Now they would be rich. Later, he would tell his Abbu how he tricked the Nawab into coming on time. He knew his Abbu would laugh and give him some money, maybe a whole mohur. With it he and Aman could buy kites and tops in the market and treat themselves to kulfi and falooda.

As Nawab Hasan Ali ate and ate, Sadiq smiled and smiled.

Illustrated by Viky Arya

Poile Sengupta

·

THE LIGHTS CHANGED

 I had meant it as a joke. A joke made up for a small boy who sold newspapers at the Janpath crossing. Every time I cycled past he would run after me, holding out the English paper and screaming out the evening's headlines in a mixture of Hindi and English. This time, I stopped by the pavement and asked for the Hindi paper. His mouth fell open. 'You mean you know Hindi?' he asked. 'Of course,' I said. 'Why? What did you think?'

He paused. 'But you look so...so angrez,' he said. 'You mean you can even read Hindi?'

'Of course I can,' I said, this time a little impatiently. 'I can speak, read and write Hindi. Hindi is one of the subjects I study in school.'

'Subjects?' he asked. How could I explain what a subject was to someone who had never been to school? 'Well, it is something...' I began, but the lights changed, and the honking behind me grew a hundredfold, and I let myself be pushed along with the rest of the traffic.

The next day he was there again, smiling at me and holding out a Hindi paper. '*Bhaiyya*,' he said, '*aap ka akhbaar. Ab bathaaiye yeh subject kya cheez hai?*' The English word sounded so strange on his tongue. It sounded like its other meaning in English—to be ruled by someone else.

'Oh it's just something to study,' I said. And then because the red light had come on, I asked him, 'Have you ever been to school?'

'Never,' he answered. And he added proudly, 'I began working when I was so high.' He measured himself against my cycle-seat. 'First my mother used

to come with me but now I can do it all alone.'

'Where is your mother now?' I asked, but then the lights changed and I was off. I heard him yell from somewhere behind me, 'She's in Meerut with...' The rest was drowned out.

'My name is Samir,' he said the next day. And very shyly he asked, 'What's yours?'

It was incredible. My bicycle wobbled. 'My name is Samir too,' I said.

'What?' His eyes lit up.

'Yes,' I grinned. 'It's another name for Hanuman, you know.'

'So now you are Samir *ek* and I'm Samir *do*,' he said triumphantly.

'Something like that,' I answered and then I held out my hand. '*Haath milao,* Samir *do!*'

His hand nestled in mine like a little bird. I could still feel its warmth as I cycled away.

The next day, he did not have his usual smile for me. 'There is trouble in Meerut,' he said. 'Many Muslims are being killed there in the riots.'

I looked at his headlines. Communal Riots, it blazed.

'But Samir...' I began.

'I'm a Muslim Samir,' he said in answer. 'And all my people are in Meerut.' His eyes filled with tears and when I touched his shoulder, he would not look up.

He was not at the crossing the following day. Nor the day after that, or ever again. And no newspaper, in English or Hindi, can tell me where my Samir *do* has gone.

Illustrated by Subir Roy

Vikram Seth

THE ELEPHANT AND THE TRAGOPAN

In Bingle Valley, broad
            and green,
            Where neither hut nor field is seen,
Where bamboo, like a distant lawn,
Is gold at dusk and flushed at dawn,
Where rhododendron forests crown
The hills, and wander halfway down
In scarlet blossom, where each year
A dozen shy black bears appear,
Where a cold river, filmed with ice,
Sustains a minor paradise,
An elephant and tragopan
Discussed their fellow creature, man.

The tragopan last week had heard
The rumour from another bird
—Most probably a quail or sparrow:
Such birds have gossip in their marrow—
That man had hatched a crazy scheme
To mar their land and dam their stream,
To flood the earth on which they stood,
And cut the woods down for their wood.
The tragopan, good-natured pheasant,
A trifle shocked by this unpleasant

Even if quite unlikely news
Had scurried off to test the views
Of his urbane and patient friend,
The elephant, who in the end
Had swung his trunk from side to side
With gravitas, and thus replied:
'Who told you? Ah, the quail—oh well,
I rather doubt—but who can tell?
I would suggest we wait and see.
Now would you care to have some tea?'
'Gnau! gnau!' the tragopan agreed.
'That is exactly what I need.
And if you have a bamboo shoot
Or fresh oak-leaves or ginseng-root—
Something that's crunchy but not prickly...
I feel like biting something quickly.'
The elephant first brewed the tea
In silence, then said carefully:
'Now let me think what I can get you.
I fear this rumour has upset you.
Your breast looks redder than before.
Do ruffle down. Here, let me pour.'
He drew a lukewarm gallon up
His trunk, and poured his friend a cup.

A week passed, and the tragopan
One morning read the news and ran
In panic down the forest floor
To meet the elephant once more.
A cub-reporter bison calf
Who wrote for Bingle Telegraph
Had just confirmed the frightful fact
In language chilling and exact.
'Here, read it!' said the tragopan,
And so the elephant began:
'Bingle. 5th April. Saturday.
Reliable informants say
That the Great Bigshot Number One
Shri Padma Bhushan Gobardhun
And the Man-Council of this state,
Intending to alleviate
The water shortage in the town
Across our ridge and ten miles down,
Have spent three cartloads of rupees
So far upon consultants' fees—
Whose task is swiftly to appraise
Efficient, cheap, and speedy ways
To dam our stream, create a lake,
And blast a tunnel through to take
Sufficient water to supply
The houses that men occupy.'

'What do you think,' the tragopan
Burst out, 'about this wicked plan
To turn our valley blue and brown?

I will not take this lying down.
I'll cluck at them. I'll flap my wings.
I tell you, I will do such things—
What they are yet I do not know,
But, take my word, I mean to show
Those odious humans what I feel.
And the Great Partridge will reveal
—That Partridge, dwelling in the sky,
Who looks down on us from on high—
He will reveal to us the way—
So kneel with me and let us pray.'

The elephant said, 'Let me think.
Before we pray, let's have a drink.
Some bamboo wine—perhaps some tea?'
'No, no,' the bird said angrily,
'I will not give in to distraction.
This isn't time for tea but action.'
The wattled horns upon his head
Stood upright in an angry red.
The elephant said nothing; he
Surveyed the landscape thoughtfully
And flapped his ears like a great fan
To cool the angry tragopan.

'It's infamous, I know,' he said,
'But we have got to use our head.
Praying may help us—who can tell?—
But they, of course, have gods as well.
I would endeavour to maintain

Our plans on a terrestrial plane.
What I suggest is we convoke
The Beastly Board of Forest Folk
For a full meeting to discuss
The worst that can occur to us.'
And so, that evening, all the creatures
—With tusks or gills or other features—
Met at the river's edge to plan
How they might outmanoeuvre man.
Gibbons and squirrels, snakes, wild dogs,
Deer and macaques, three types of frogs,
Porcupines, eagles, trout, wagtails,
Civet cats, sparrows, bears and quails,
Bloodsucking leeches, mild-eyed newts,
And leopards in their spotted suits—
Stated their stances, asked their questions,
And made their manifold suggestions.
Some predators drooled at the sight,
But did not act on appetite.
The leopards did not kill the deer.
The smaller birds evinced no fear.
Each eagle claw sat in its glove.
The mood was truce, if not quite love.
At meetings of the Beastly Board
Eating each other was outlawed.

The arguments grew sharp and heated.
Some views advanced, and some retreated.
Some feared to starve, and some to drown.
Some said they should attack the town.

The trout said they were unconcerned
If the whole bamboo forest burned
So long as they had space to swim.
The mynahs joked, the boars looked grim.
They talked for hours, and at the close
At last the elephant arose,
And with a modest trumpet-call
Drew the attention of them all:

'O Beasts of Bingle gathered round,
Though in our search for common ground
I would not dream of unanimity
I hope our views may reach proximity.
I speak to you as one whose clan
Has served and therefore studied man.
He is a creature mild and vicious,
Practical-minded and capricious,
Loving and brutal, sane and mad,
The good as puzzling as the bad.
The sticky centre of this mess
Is an uneasy selfishness.
He rips our flesh and tears our skin
For cloth without, for food within.
The leopard's spots are his to wear.
Our ivory unknots his hair.
The tragopan falls to his gun.
He shoots the flying fox for fun.
The black bear dances to his whim.
My own tame cousins slave for him.
Yet we who give him work and food

Have never earned his gratitude.
He grasps our substance as of right
To quench and spur his appetite,
Nor will he grant us truce or grace
To rest secure in any place.
Sometimes he worships us as Gods
Or sings of us at Eisteddfods,
Or fashions fables, myths, and stories
To celebrate our deeds and glories.
And yet, despite this fertile fuss,
When has he truly cared for us?
He sees the planet as his fief
Where every hair or drop or leaf
Or seed or blade or grain of sand
Is destined for his mouth or hand.
If he is thirsty, we must thirst—
For of all creatures, man comes first.
If he needs room, then we must fly;
And if he hungers, we must die.
 Think what will happen, when
  his scheme
To tame our valley and our stream
Begins to thrust its way across
These gentle slopes of fern and moss
With axe, explosive, and machine.
Since rhododendron logs burn green
They'll all be chopped for firewood—
Or logged and smuggled out for good.
As every bird and mammal knows,
When the road comes, the forest goes.

And let me say this to the trout—
The bamboo will be slashed, no doubt,
And what the tragopan and I
Delight to eat, will burn and die.
But what will happen to your stream?
Before the reservoir, your dream
Of endless space, can come about,
The soot and filth will snuff you out.
What tolls for us is your own bell.
And similarly let me tell
The leopards who may fancy here
A forestful of fleeing deer—
After your happy, passing slaughter,
You too will have to flee from water.
You will be homeless, like us all.
It is this fate we must forestall.
So let me say to every single
Endangered denizen of Bingle:
We must unite in fur and feather—
For we will live or die together.'

All this made such enormous sense
That all except the rather dense
Grey peacock-pheasants burst out cheering.
The peacock-pheasants, after hearing
The riotous applause die down,
Asked, with an idiotic frown:
 'But what is it we plan to do?'
 A bison calf remarked: 'I knew
  Those peacock-pheasants

were half-witted.'
And everybody joshed and twitted
The silly birds till they were dumb.
'How typical! How troublesome!'
A monkey said: 'What awful taste!
How graceless and how brazen-faced,
When all of us are clapping paws,
To undermine our joint applause.'
Oddly, the elephant was the beast
Who of them all was put out least.
He flapped his ears and bowed his head.
'The pheasants have a point,' he said.

'Unfortunately,' he went on,
'The days of beastly strength are gone.
We don't have mankind on the run.
That's why he's done what he has done.
We can't, as someone here suggested,
Burn down the town. We'd be arrested.
Or maimed or shot or even eaten.
But I will not accept we're beaten.
Someone suggested that we flee
And set up our community
In some far valley where no man
Has ever trod—or ever can.
Sweet to the mind though it may seem,
This is, alas, an idle dream—
For nowhere lies beyond man's reach
To mar and burn and flood and leach.
A distant valley is indeed

No sanctuary from his greed.
Besides, the beasts already there
Will fight with us for food and air.
No, we must struggle for this land
Where we have stood and where we stand.
What I suggest is that we go
To the Great Bigshot down below
And show him how self-interest
And what his conscience says is best
Both tell him 'Let the valley be.'
Who knows—perhaps he may agree,
If nothing else, to hear us out.
But we must take, without a doubt,
Firm data to support our prayer—
And in addition must prepare
Some other scheme by which he can
Ensure more water gets to man—
For, by the twitching of my trunk,
Without that we'll be truly sunk.'

And so it happened that a rally
Meandered forth from Bingle Valley
A few days later, up and down
The hills towards the human town.
With trumpet, cackle, grunt and hoot
They harmonized along their route,
And 'Long live Bingladesh' was heard
From snout of beast and beak of bird.
'Protect our spots,' the leopards growled;
While the wild dogs and gibbons howled:

'Redress our sad and sorry tale,
The tragedy of Bingle Vale.'
And there, red-breasted in the van,
Cluck-clucked the gallant tragopan—
Raised high upon the elephant's neck,
And guiding him by prod and peck.
The only absentees, the trout,
Were much relieved to slither out.
They asked: 'How can we wet our gills
Clambering up and down those hills?
The journey will be far too taxing;
We'd rather spend the time relaxing.
We'll guard the valley while you plead.'
'All right,' the other beasts agreed.

Meanwhile from fields and gates and doors
The villagers came out in scores
To see the cavalcade go by.
Some held their children shoulder-high
While others clutched a bow or gun
And dreamed of pork or venison—
But none had seen or even heard
Of such a horde of beast and bird,
And not a bullet or an arrow
Touched the least feather of a sparrow.
So stunned and stupefied were they,
They even cheered them on the way
Or joined them on the route to town—
Where the Great Bigshot with a frown
Said to his Ministers, 'Look here!

What is this thing that's
        drawing near?
What is this beastly
        ragtag army—
Have I gone blind? Or am I barmy?—'

'Yes, yes, Sir—' said the Number Two.
'I mean, no, no, Sir—what to do?
They've not gone through the proper channels.
The Protocol Protection Panels
Have no idea who they are.
Nor does the Riffraff Registrar.
It's possible they don't exist.'
'Well,' said the Bigshot, getting pissed,
'Exist or not, they're getting near.
And you'll be Number Twelve, I fear,
Unless you find out what the fuss
Is all about, and tender us
Advice on what to say and do.
And think. And be. Now off with you.'
The Number Two was almost crying.
He rushed off with his shirt-tails flying,
Without a cummerbund or hat,
And flew back in a minute flat.

'Oh, Bigshot, Sir, thanks to your grace,
By which I'm here in second place,
Thanks to your wisdom and your power
Which grows in glory by the hour,
Thanks to the faith you've placed in me,

Which gives me strength to hear and see,
Thanks to—' 'Yes, yes,' the Bigshot said,
'Thanks to my power to cut you dead,
What is it you have come to learn?'
'Sir, Sir, they plan to overturn
Your orders, Sir, to dam up Bingle.
And, Sir, I saw some pressmen mingle
With the parade to interview
A clouded leopard and a shrew.
The beasts are all against your plan.
The worst of them's the tragopan.
His eyes are fierce, his breast is red.
He wears a wattle on his head.
He looks so angry I've a hunch
That he's the leader of the bunch.
And when I met them, they weren't far—
Oh Sir—oh no, Sir—here they are!'

For now a hoolock gibbon's paw
Was battering on the Bigshot's door
And animals from far and wide
Were crowding in on every side.
'Save Bingle Valley!' rose the cry;
'For Bingle let us do or die.'
'Wait!' screamed the Bigshot in a tizzy.
'Wait! Wait! You can't come in. I'm busy.
I'm the Great Bigshot Number One,
Shri Padma Bhushan Gobardhun.
I rule by popular anointment.
You have to meet me by appointment.'

'What nonsense!' cried the tragopan:
'You try to stop us if you can.'
The Bigshot sensed their resolution,
And turned from awe to elocution.
'Dear friends,' he said, 'regretfully,
The matter isn't up to me.
What the Man-Council has decreed
Is not for me to supersede.
It's true I, so to speak, presided.
But all—and none—of us decided.
That is the doctrine, don't you see,
Of joint responsibility.
But if next year in early fall
You fill, in seven copies, all
The forms that deal with such a case
And bring them over to my place
Together with the filing fees
And three translations in Chinese,
The Council, at my instigation,
May give them due consideration.
Meanwhile, my friends, since you are here
A little early in the year
—No fault of yours, of course, but still,
It's not the best of times—I will
Invite you to a mighty feast
Where every bird and every beast
Will sup on simply super food;
And later, if you're in the mood,
Please come to hear the speech I'm due
To give this evening at the zoo.'

At this pathetic tactless bribe
A sound rose from the beastly tribe
So threatening that the Bigshot trembled
And said to all who were assembled:
'My beastly comrades, bear with me.
You are upset, as I can see.
I meant the stadium, not the zoo.'
He gestured to his Number Two
Who scrawled a memo in his diary.
'Perhaps an innocent inquiry,'
The elephant said, 'may clear the air.
Please tell us all, were you aware,
Sir Bigshot, when you spoke just now,
That even if we did somehow
Fill out your forms and pay your fees,
Your cure would postdate our disease?
Before next fall our valley would
Have disappeared for ill or good.
The remedy that you suggest,
It might be thought, is not the best.'

A crafty look appeared upon
The Bigshot's face, and then was gone.
'Of course, my friends, it slipped
        my mind.
But then, these days, I often find
I have so many files to read,
So many seminars to lead,
So many meetings to attend,
        So many talks, that in the end

A minor fact or two slips by.
But, elephant, both you and I
Appear to understand the world.'
And here the Bigshot's fingers
        curled
Around a little golden ring.
'This vast unwieldy gathering,
Dear Elephant, is not the place
Where we can reason, face to face,
About what can or should be done.
We should discuss this one on one.
To be quite frank, your deputation
Has not filled me with fond elation.
Tell them to leave; I'll close the door,
And we'll continue as before.'

Although the other beasts agreed,
The elephant declared: 'I'll need
My secretary and mahout
To help me sort this matter out.
Like all the rest, he's left the room,
But he can come back, I presume.
There's two of you and one of me—
So I expect that you'll agree.'
The Bigshot nodded: 'Call the man.'
Quick as a quack the tragopan
Opened the door and strutted in
To greet his buddy with a grin.
The Bigshot and his Number Two
Scowled as they murmured, 'How d'you do?'

Tea came; the Bigshot looked benign.
'Milk?' 'Thanks.' 'And sugar?' 'One is fine.'
'It's not too strong?' 'I like mine weak.'
At last the moment came to speak.
'You see, good beasts,' the Bigshot said,
'We need your water—or we're dead.
It's for the people that I act.
The town must drink, and that's a fact.
Believe me, all your agitation
Will only lead to worse frustration.
Go back, dear beasts, to Bingle now.
We'll relocate you all somehow
In quarters of a certain size.'
He yawned, and rolled his little eyes.

Immediately, the tragopan
Pulled out his papers, and began,
With fact and query and suggestion,
To give the Bigshot indigestion.
'You say the town is short of water,
Yet at the wedding of your daughter
The whole municipal supply
Was poured upon your lawns. Well, why?
And why is it that Minister's Hill
And Babu's Barrow drink their fill
Through every season, dry or wet,
When all the common people get
Is water on alternate days?
At least, that's what my data says,
And every figure has been checked.

So, Bigshot, wouldn't you expect
A radical redistribution
Would help provide a just solution?'

The Bigshot's placid face grew red.
He turned to Number Two and said
In a low voice: 'This agitator
Is dangerous. Deal with him later.'
Then, turning to the elephant,
He murmured sweetly, 'I'll be blunt.
Your friend's suggestion is quite charming,
But his naïveté's alarming.
Redistribute it night and day,
Redistribute it all away,
Ration each drop, and you'll still find
Demand will leave supply behind.'

The elephant first sipped his tea,
Then ate a biscuit leisuredly,
Then shook his head from side to side,
And, having cleared his trunk, replied:
'Well, even as regards supply,
I do not see the reason why
You do not use what lies to hand
Before you try to dam our land.
Even my short walk through this town
Shows me how everything's run down
During your long administration.
Your pipes cry out for renovation.
Your storage tanks corrode and leak;

The valves are loose, the washers weak.
I've seen the water gushing out
From every reservoir and spout.
Repair them: it will cost far less
Than driving us to homelessness
By blasting tunnels through our hills
And bloating your construction bills.
But that's just one of many things:
Plant trees; revive your wells and springs.
Guide from your roofs the monsoon rain
Into great tanks to use again.
Reduce your runoff and your waste
Rather than with unholy haste
Destroying beauty which, once gone,
The world will never look upon.'
The elephant, now overcome
With deep emotion, brushed a crumb
Of chocolate biscuit off his brow.

'Dear chap,' the Bigshot said, 'Somehow
I think you fail to comprehend
What really matters in the end.
The operative word is Votes,
And next to that comes Rupee-notes.
Your plans do not appeal to me
Because, dear chap, I fail to see
How they will help me gather either.'
He giggled, then continued: 'Neither
The charming cheques that generous firms
With whom the Council comes to terms

—Who wish to dam or log or clear
Or build—will come to me, I fear,
Nor votes from those who think my schemes
Will satisfy their thirsty dreams.
It's not just water that must funnel
Out of the hills through Bingle Tunnel.
Do animals have funds or votes—
Or anything but vocal throats?
Will you help me get re-elected?
You're speechless? Just as I suspected.
I've tried to talk things out with you.
Now I will tell you what to do:
Lift up your stupid trunk and sign
This waiver on the dotted line.
Give up all rights in Bingle Vale
For fur or feather, tusk or tail.
Sadly, since you're now in the know,
I can't afford to let you go.
Your friend will never leave this room.
The tragopan has found his tomb.
As for yourself, my Number Two
Will soon escort you to the zoo.
From this the other beasts will learn
Your lands are ours to slash and burn
And anyone defying man
Will be a second tragopan.'
He giggled with delight, and padded
His cheeks with air, and gently added:
'But if you go cahoots with me
I'll spare your friend and set you free.'

He stroked his ring. 'And I'll
    make sure
You'll be—let's say—provided for.'
Before you could say 'Pheasant stew'
The servile hands of Number Two
Grasped the bird's collar in a vice.
The elephant went cold as ice
To see his friend cry out in terror.
He would have signed the form in error
Had not the tragopan cried out:
'Don't sign. Gock, Gock.' And at his shout
The Bigshot's son came running in
And struck the henchman on the chin.

While the foiled killer squealed and glared,
For a long time the Smallfry stared
With indignation at his father.
'Papa—' he said, 'I would much
    rather
Give up my place as Number Three
Than countenance such treachery.
Why can't we let the valley live?
Those who succeed us won't forgive
The Rape of Bingle. I recall,'
The Smallfry sighed, 'when I was small
You used to take me walking there
With Mama in the open air.
For me, a dusty city boy,
It was a dream of peace and joy.
Along safe paths we'd walk; a deer

Might unexpectedly appear
Among the bamboos and the moss
And raise its velvet ears and toss
Its startled head and bound away.
Once I saw leopard cubs at play
And heard the mother's warning cough
Before you quickly marched me off.
Until this day there's not a single
House or hut or field in Bingle.
How many worlds like this remain
To free our hearts from noise and pain?
And is this lovely fragile vision
To be destroyed by your decision?
And do you now propose to make
A tunnel, dam, and pleasure lake
With caravans and motorboats
And tourists at each others' throats,
Loudspeakers, shops, high-tension wires,
And ferris wheels and forest fires?
As the roads come, the trees will go.
Do villagers round Bingle know
What's going to happen to their lands?
Are they too eating from your hands?
I had gone snorkelling on the day
The Council met and signed away
The Bingle Bills. I know you signed—
But why can you not change your mind?
You talk of sacrifice and glory.
Your actions tell a different story.
Do you expect me to respect you—

Or decent folk not to detect you?
Where you have crept, must mankind crawl,
Feared, hated, and despised by all?
Don't sign, dear Elephant, don't sign.
Don't toe my wretched father's line.
Dear Tragopan, do not despair.
Don't yield the struggle in mid-air.
I'll help your cause. And as for you—'
(He turned towards the Number Two)
'This time your chin, next time your head—,'
Rubbing his fists, the Smallfry said.

The Number Two lay on the ground.
A snivelling, grovelling, snarling sound
Oozed from his throat. The Bigshot stood
As rigid as a block of wood.
He tried to speak; no words came out.
Then with an eerie strangled shout
He uttered: 'You malignant pup!
Is this the way I've brought you up?
Where did you learn your blubbery blabbering?
Your jelly-livered jungle-jabbering?
Your education's made you weak—
A no-good, nattering nature-freak
Who's snorkelled half his life away.
Who asked you to go off that day?
You've been brought up in privilege
With Coca Cola in your fridge
And litchis in and out of season.
How dare you now descend to treason?

One day all this would have been yours—
These antlers and these heads of boars,
This office and these silver plates,
These luminous glass paperweights,
My voting bank, my Number Game,
My files, my fortune, and my fame.
I had a dream my only son
Would follow me as Number One.
I had been grooming you to be
A Bigger Bigshot after me.
You might have been a higher hero
And risen to be Number Zero—
But now, get out! You're in disgrace,'
He said, and struck the Smallfry's face.

The Smallfry, bleeding from the nose,
Fell, and the Number Two arose,
And slobbering over the Bigshot's hand
Called him the saviour of the land.
At this, the elephant got mad
And, putting down the pen he had
Clasped in his trunk to sign, instead
Poured the whole teapot on their head.
The water in a boiling arc
Splashed down upon its double-mark.
The Bigshot and his henchman howled.
The tragopan gock-gocked and scowled:
'You wanted water; here's your share.'
Then guards came in from everywhere—
And animals came in as well—

All was confusion and pell-mell
While news-reporters clicked and
    whirred
At limb of man and wing of bird.
The elephant stayed very still.
The tragopan rushed round—until,
Provoked by a pernicious peck,
The Bigshot wrung its little neck.

The tragopan collapsed and cried
'Gock, gock!' and rolled his eyes and died.
He died before he comprehended
His transient span on earth had ended—
Nor could he raise a plaintive cry
To the Great Partridge in the sky
Whose head is wrapped in golden gauze
To take his spirit in His claws.

What happened happened very fast.
The mêlée was put down at last.
The Smallfry cried out when he found
The pheasant stretched out on the ground.
The Bigshot too began repenting
When he saw everyone lamenting
The martyr's selfless sacrifice.
He had the body laid on ice,
Draped in the state flag, and arrayed
With chevron, scutcheon, and cockade—
And all the townsfolk came to scan
The features of the tragopan.

Four buglers played 'Abide with Me';
Four matrons wept on a settee;
Four brigadiers with visage grim
Threw cornflakes and puffed rice on him;
Four schoolgirls robbed the tragopan
Of feathers for a talisman;
And everyone stood round and kept
Long vigil while the hero slept.

A long, alas, a final sleep!
O, Elephant, long may you weep.
O, Elephant, long may you mourn.
This is a night that knows no dawn.
Ah! every Bingle eye is blurred
With sorrow for its hero-bird
And every Bingle heart in grief
Turns to its fellow for relief.
Alas for Bingle! Who will lead
The struggle in its hour of need?
Is it the grief-bowed elephant
Who now must bear the beastly brunt?
Or will the gallant martyr-bird
In death, if not in life, be heard?
Dare the egregious Bigshot mock
The cry, 'Save Bingle! Gock, gock, gock!'
And can a ghostly Tragopan
Help to attain a Bingle Ban?

For it undoubtedly was true
That suddenly the whole state knew

Of Bingle Valley and the trek
That ended in the fatal peck,
And panegyrics to the pheasant
In prose and verse were omnipresent.
Suggestions for a cenotaph
Appeared in Bingle Telegraph;
And several human papers too
Discussed the matter through and through.
The water problem in the state
Became a topic for debate.
The Bigshot, struggling with the flood,
Was splashed with editorial mud.
Then intellectuals began
To analyse the tragopan.
Was he a hothead or a martyr?
A compromiser or a tartar?
A balanced and strategic planner
Or an unthinking project-banner?
It seemed that nobody could tell.
And maybe that was just as well—
For mystery matched with eccentricity
Provides the grist for great publicity,
And myths of flexible dimension
Are apt to call forth less dissension.

This is a tale without a moral.
I hope the reader will not quarrel

About this minor missing link.
But if he likes them, he can think
Of five or seven that will do
As quasi-morals; here are two:
　　　The first is that you never know
Just when your luck may break, and so
You may as well work for your cause
Even without overt applause;
You might, in time, achieve your ends.
　　　The second is that you'll find friends
In the most unexpected places,
Hidden among unfriendly faces—
For Smallfry swim in every pond,
Even the Doldrums of Despond.

And so I'll end the story here.
What is to come is still unclear.
Whether the fates will smile or frown,
And Bingle Vale survive or drown,
I do not know and cannot say;
Indeed, perhaps, I never may.
I hope, of course, the beasts we've met
Will save their hidden valley, yet
The resolution of their plight
Is for the world, not me,
　　　to write.

Illustrated by Atanu Roy

Kalpana Swaminathan

■

FROM

THE TRUE ADVENTURES OF PRINCE TEENTANG

Once upon a time, not so very long ago, there was born in the kingdom of Tintoor, a prince who had three legs. His arrival was greeted with great rejoicing, for though the king and the queen had five other children, they were ordinary children with two legs each. The proud parents named the new prince Teentang.

The Queen declared a National Holiday Week and the people were commanded to make merry. As the poor folk of Tintoor seldom had a holiday, they needed no second bidding, and downed their tools with great haste lest the Queen change her mind. Further, in a rare burst of generosity, the King ordered wages to be raised by one coin, minimizing his rashness however, by making this coin the smallest of the realm. The people of Tintoor spent that extra coin (and several more besides) in journeying to the Palace gates to catch a glimpse of their new prince.

It was the custom in that kingdom to display a life-size portrait of every new-born Royal Baby on the Palace gates. Now you must know that the portrait of Teentang was one of a set of twelve gifted to Their Royal Majesties on their wedding day by the Palace Artist, for it was usual for all Royal Babies to be painted well in advance of their arrival. The Palace Artist had been congratulated on the first five portraits which were considered very good likenesses. This was perfectly true because one baby looks very much like another, unless he happens to be special, like Teentang. When he heard of the arrival of Teentang, the Palace Artist (who had not predicted the baby's third leg) trembled for his neck—and he would have lost it too—but for his daughter, who stole into the Portrait Gallery in the dead of night, and with infinite resource, painted a blanket of royal blue all around Teentang's chubby legs.

When the portrait was unveiled the next morning, there was loud acclaim, for the royal baby wrapped in his blue blanket, was a perfect likeness of Teentang. The King gave the Artist a whole bushel of coal (taking the tally up to a ton and a half). Palace rates were a bushel a portrait—more generous monarchs would have paid in gold. The Artist, his neck secure, wheeled the coal home jauntily till he caught sight of his daughter waiting eagerly at the gate. Poor girl! She had been hoping for grain this time! With a heavy sigh, she tipped the barrow of useless coal into the last of their coal bins—what indeed is the use of lighting a stove when you have nothing to cook on it?

Teentang grows up in the Palace rebelling against his nappies of Benaras silk, his crystal bottle of nectar and his golden hoop. He prefers the patched pants that belong to the Gardener's Boy—with an extra leg sewn on, these are a great improvement on the Palace wardrobe. His tutors fail to teach him the alphabet, and the King sends for the Learned Professors. But these venerable men and women, touched by a sunbeam, dance out of the Palace to fly a kite on Hawa Hill. Teentang, saddened by the joy of the world outside the Palace, resolves to discover the world for himself.

When the King and the Queen hear that Teentang has driven away the Learned Professors without learning to add, they are furious. They issue a Royal Edict that Teentang is to be left Severely Alone. They also bestow on Teentang a new title: from now on he will be called His Royal Liability. The King and the Queen summon Parliament the very next morning to decide What Must Be Done About His Royal Liability.

Meanwhile in the Palace, Parliament did not adjourn for lunch, but the people ate out of little bags and tin boxes, while the King, the Queen and their Ministers who could not eat out of paper bags because of Dignity, grew hungrier, and angrier. The Queen was growing giddy from the delicious whiffs that wafted up to her. Finally, as the Palace Carpenter in the fourth row peeled an orange, its sharp scent quite vanquished the Queen and she fainted with a loud thud.

In the confusion that followed, with the ladies-in-waiting sprinkling water (with the garden hose, which was handy, just outside the window on the lawn), and four stout stretcher-bearers being recruited from the cooks in the back row, there were a good many paper bags abandoned on the benches, and these were deftly retrieved by the Prime Minister, a man renowned for his strategy.

The King and his Cabinet refreshed themselves with several furtive bites (unobserved except by the Gardener's Boy, who lived to tell the tale to his grandchildren).

Greatly refreshed, the King addressed himself to the business at hand with verve. Flinging his velvet train over his left shoulder, he banged the sceptre on his throne of beaten gold.

'We have decided!' he roared.

Seventy thousand paper bags immediately stopped rustling. The Chancellor dropped the pin he had been picking his teeth with, and the entire assembly heard it fall.

'We have decided,' repeated the King, in a sort of friendly growl, 'what must be done about His Royal Liability. As it seems impossible for him to learn his letters, we have decided that he must be taught a Trade!'

There was tremendous applause. Several tradesmen were seen to mop their brows, loosen their collars and check whether their heads were firmly glued on.

The Prime Minister now rose to read the list of Trades. There were thirty-five thousand Trades in all, so everybody had a comfortable nap except the Prime Minister, and the thirty-five thousand Tradesmen who had to keep awake to answer the roll-call or forfeit their necks.

'Now, Your Majesty,' said the Prime Minister, with a gentle prod, as the thirty-five thousandth Tradesman sat down, 'which of these Trades do you choose for His Royal Liability?'

The King, who had awakened all rosy and beneficent, took a little time to consider. 'Let the Prince choose!' he cried expansively. 'Produce him!'

Fifty courtiers rushed off in fifty directions to find Teentang. They spent an hour searching for him, but of course, Teentang was nowhere to be found. They wasted another half an hour drawing lots to decide who should inform the King that he was one Liability short.

'Whaa-aa-aat!' roared the King. The Prime Minister grew pale in consternation and summoned the Chief of Police.

The Chief of Police— Dagad was his name—was a swaggering giant of a man with the most tremendous moustachios. Criminals turned white and shrivelled under his steely gaze. His policemen obeyed him blindly, by instinct. Nobody, within living memory, had heard him speak a word, which was just as well, for this enormous man had a tiny treble voice more fit for a tired cat than a policeman. His mother had lavished Throat Pastilles and Strengthening Foods on him: they strengthened everything about him except his voice. In despair, she sent him to the zoo, for she had begged the Lion to take him on as an apprentice. The Lion was so disgusted with the mew that the boy produced in response to his Best Roar that he buffeted him hard with his paw. This enraged Dagad who picked up the Lion by his mane and shook him so violently that his old yellow teeth rattled in his jaws. Nobody can tell what would have happened next if the Zoo Keeper (who had an old score to settle with the Lion) had not come running with the hose and doused the two heroes completely. The vanquished Lion regarded his apprentice with new respect, for Lions always admire courage even when they lack it themselves. The Keeper was so thrilled to see the Lion discomfited that he commended Dagad's strength and courage publicly, and the Police snapped him up at once as a recruit.

By dint of his dauntless deeds, and also his moustachios, Dagad soon became Chief. His voice was one of the best kept secrets in the kingdom. At this moment his silence stood him in good stead.

From the chapters 'Introducing Teentang' and 'What Happened in Parliament'

Illustrated by Bindia Thapar

NOTES ON WRITERS AND TRANSLATORS

Paro Anand 1957– An accomplished storyteller, Anand is the recipient of the 1998 Award for Significant Contribution to Children's Literature from the Russian Centre for Science and Culture. Her fiction focuses on issues that confront children and teenagers. Among her books are *Pepper the Capuchin Monkey and Other Stories* (1992); *The Little Bird* (1993); *Born to Lead* (1994) and *School Soup* (1996).

Margaret Bhatty 1930– Author and freelance journalist, retired school and college teacher, Bhatty has written extensively for children. Her books include *The Circus Boy; The Secret of the Sickle Moon Mountain; The Adventures of Bhim the Bold; Himalayan Holiday* and *The Family at Paangar Pani.* In 1982 she won the first prize in the BBC World Service international short story competition.

Pankaj Bisht 1946– A Hindi fiction writer, Bisht has written two novels and five short story collections. He has also written a few short stories for children. *Bholu and Golu* is his only novel for children.

Ruskin Bond 1934– Bond, probably India's best-known writer in English for children, grew up in Jamnagar, Dehradun, New Delhi and Simla. As a young man, he spent four years in the Channel Islands and London. He returned to India in 1955, and has never left the country since then. His first novel, *The Room on the Roof,* received the John Llewellyn Rhys Prize, awarded to a Commonwealth writer under thirty, for 'a work of outstanding literary merit'. He received the Sahitya Akademi Award in 1993, and the Padma Shri in 1999. He lives in Landour, Mussoorie, with his extended family. He has written over thirty stories for children, besides a novel, *The Adventures of Rusty* which has been translated into many Indian languages.

Anita Desai 1937– Desai is one of India's best-known contemporary writers. *The Village by the Sea* (1982), winner of the *Guardian* Award for Children's Fiction, was serialized by BBC Television in 1991. She has also written *The Peacock Garden* (1974) and *Cat on a Houseboat* (1976) for children. She is Professor of Writing at the Massachusetts Institute of Technology at Cambridge.

Shashi Deshpande Deshpande has written four books for children besides many novels and stories for adults. *The Narayanpur Incident* has been translated into German.

Mahasweta Devi 1926– A prolific and best-selling author in Bengali, Mahasweta Devi has written novels, short stories, children's stories and plays. A deeply committed social activist she has been working with and for tribals and marginalized communities. Her work includes *Mother of 1084: A Novel; Breast Stories: Draupadi; Breast-Giver; Behind the Bodice* and *Our Non-Veg Cow and Other Stories.*

Shama Futehally 1952– Futehally studied English at the universities of Bombay and Leeds. Her novels include *Tara Lane* (1993); *Reaching Bombay Central* (forthcoming) and a translation of Meera's bhajans *In the Dark of the Heart* (1994). She has co-edited a book of short stories for children *Sorry, Best Friend!* (1997) which also includes a story by her.

Mala Marwah 1948– Writer and painter, Marwah studied in Calcutta and Mussoorie. She spent three years in Berkeley at the California College of Arts and Crafts. The children's magazine *Target* carried her illustrated stories and features regularly. Her other published work includes writing on modern Indian art, short stories and poetry. She is currently working on a picture gallery of Indian art for children.

Arvind Krishan Mehrotra 1947– Poet and critic, Mehrotra's books include *The Transfiguring Places* (1998) and *The Absent Traveller: Prakrit Love Poetry from the Gathasaptasati* (1991), both published by Ravi Dayal. He has edited the *Oxford India Anthology of Twelve Modern Indian Poets* (1992). He lives in Dehradun and Allahabad.

Dhan Gopal Mukerji 1890–1936 Mukerji's novel *Gay-Neck: The Story of a Pigeon* (1927) is the only Indian book to win the Newbery Medal given for an outstanding literary work for children. Mukerji migrated to America at the age of nineteen and spent the rest of his life there. His books include *Kari, the Elephant* (1922), *Jungle Beasts and Men* (1923), *Hari, the Jungle Lad* (1924), *Ghond, the Hunter* (1928), *The Chief of the Herd* (1929) and *Fierce-Face: The Story of a Tiger* (1936).

Meenakshi Mukherjee has translated two children's books: Mahasweta Devi's *Etoa Munda Won the Battle* published by the National Book Trust and the classic from Bengali, *Kheerer Putul,* by Abanindranath Tagore, titled *The Cheese Doll* in English. Mukherjee has taught English in several universities in India, Australia and the United States. Her books of literary criticism include *The Twice-Born Fiction (1971); Realism and Reality: The Novel and Society in India* (1985) and *The Perishable Empire. Another India*, co-edited by her and Nissim Ezekiel was published by Penguin India in 1990.

R.K. Narayan 1906–2001 *Swami and Friends* (1935), Narayan's first novel, was hailed by Graham Greene as a 'book in ten thousand'. Among his other novels are *The Bachelor of Arts* (1937); *The Dark Room* (1938); *The Guide*

(1958) and *The Man-eater of Malgudi* (1962). Besides six collections of short stories, Narayan published two travel books, five collections of essays, translations of Indian epics and myths, and a memoir, *My Days*. In 1980 Narayan was awarded the A.C. Benson Medal by the Royal Society of Literature and was made an honorary member of the American Academy and Institute of Arts and Letters. In 2000 he was conferred the Padma Vibhushan.

Premchand 1880-1936 Premchand was the pen-name of Dhanpat Rai. He is known as the creator of the short story as well as the realistic novel in both Hindi and Urdu and is acknowledged as one of modern India's foremost writers. Drawn to the freedom struggle, his writing for children reflects his vision of a harmonious India.

Sara Rai Rai has written a collection of short stories in Hindi, *Ababeel Ki Uraan*, and translated and edited a book of post-Independence Hindi short stories, *The Golden Waist-Chain* (1990), besides editing a collection of regional fiction, *Imaging the Other*. She has also translated two novels for children: Pankaj Bisht's *Bholu and Golu* and Shrilal Shukla's *Babbarsingh and his Friends*. She has received several awards for translation.

Shanta Rameshwar Rao 1924- Rao worked as a schoolteacher and in 1961 started her own school inspired by educationists like Mme Montessori, but mainly by the teachings of Jiddu Krishnamurti. She has written several books for children. Her books include *The Children's Mahabharata* (1968), *Tales of Ancient India* (1960), *Seethu* (1980) and *Children of God* (1991).

Hemangini Ranade 1932- Ranade worked in AIR for more than three decades producing women's and children's programmes. She has published many short stories in Hindi and Gujarati.

Satyajit Ray 1921-92 Film director, writer, translator, illustrator, designer and composer, Ray was also a prolific writer of short stories, novellas, poems, limericks, essays, and puzzles in Bengali. His unforgettable creations are Feluda, the sleuth and Professor Shonku, the scientist. He illustrated his own works and designed all the book ttd several foreign languages.

Salman Rushdie 1947- Author of *Midnight's Children* (1981) and *The Satanic Verses* (1988) amongst other work. Rushdie has won a number of literary prizes, including the Booker Prize in 1981 and the Whitbread Prize for the best novel of 1988. *Haroun and the Sea of Stories* (1990) is his only book for children.

Bhisham Sahni 1915- Sahni's work includes several novels, plays, short stories, a biography of his late brother, Balraj Sahni and a book of essays. His books have been translated into English and several Indian and foreign languages. He received the Sahitya Akademi Award for his novel *Tamas* in 1976 and was conferred the Padma Bhushan in 1998.

Poile Sengupta 1948– Fiction writer, poet, columnist and playwright, Sengupta has taught English in several universities. Her work includes many books for children: *The Exquisite Balance* (1987); award winner in the UNICEF-CBT competition, *The Way to My Friend's House* (1988); *The Story of the Road* (1993); *The Clever Carpenter and Other Stories* (1997) and *Waterflowers* (2000). She also writes textbooks for schoolchildren.

Subhadra Sen Gupta 1952– Sen Gupta's popular works of historical fiction are fast-paced adventure stories or mysteries mostly set in the Mughal period, the reigns of Emperor Ashoka and Krishnadeva Raya. Her books include *The Sword of Dara Shikoh* (1992); *Mystery of the House of Pigeons* (1993) which was made into a television serial in Hindi *Khoj Khazana Khoj* (1997); *Bishnu, the Dhobi Singer* (1994); *Bishnu Sings Again* (1998); *History, Mystery, Dal & Biryani* (2000) and *Jahanara: Diary of a Princess* (2001).

Vikram Seth 1952– Seth's books include *From Heaven Lake* (1983), an account of his travels through Sinkiang and Tibet which won the 1983 Thomas Cook Travel Book Award; *The Golden Gate: A Novel in Verse* (1986); *A Suitable Boy* (1993); *An Equal Music* (1999) and a book of animal fables in verse for children, *Beastly Tales from Here and There* (1991).

Khushwant Singh 1915– Singh is one of India's best-known columnists. Among his books are a two-volume *History of the Sikhs*, several works of fiction—including the novels *Train to Pakistan, Delhi* and *The Company of Women*—an autobiography, *Truth, Love and a Little Malice,* and a number of translated works.

Kalpana Swaminathan 1956– A paediatric surgeon and writer, Swaminathan has written both for adults and children. Her work for adults includes an anthology of short stories, *Cryptic Death* (1997); a novel, *Ambrosia for Afters* (forthcoming), and for children, *The True Adventures of Prince Teentang* (1993); *Dattatray's Dinosaur* (1994); *Ordinary Mr Pai* (1999); *The Weekday Sisters* (2002) and *Gavial Avial* (2002). She shares the pseudonym Kalpish Ratna with Ishrat Syed and their writings on science, the arts and literature appear in several national newspapers and magazines.

NOTES ON ILLUSTRATORS

Viky Arya Arya obtained her Masters in Fine Arts from Banaras Hindu University. She has conceptualized and developed many national and multimedia campaigns on child-related subjects, some of which have received national and international awards. She has illustrated several books for children. In 2002 she received the NCERT National Award for illustration.

Suddhasattwa Basu 1956- Painter, illustrator and animation film-maker, Basu studied at the College of Art, Calcutta. He is one of the foremost illustrators of children's books. Among the books he has illustrated and designed are Khushwant Singh's *Nature Watch*, Ruskin Bond's *To Live in Magic* and V. Sulaiman's *The Homecoming*.

Pulak Biswas 1941- Pioneering illustrator and painter, Biswas has been associated with all the leading publishing houses for children in India, and he has also worked for publishers in the United States, Austria and Germany. He was awarded the Grand Honorary Diploma in the Biennale of Illustrations, Bratislava, in 1967.

Sujasha Dasgupta 1964- A graduate of the College of Art, Delhi, Dasgupta has worked as a freelance illustrator for the last sixteen years with all the leading publishing houses and magazines, including Katha, the Children's Book Trust, National Book Trust, Ratna Sagar, Scholastic India, and the popular children's magazine *Children's World*.

Neeta Gangopadhya 1963- A graduate of the College of Art, Delhi, Gangopadhya has illustrated several books for children for the Children's Book Trust, National Book Trust, Ratna Sagar, Frank Brothers, Scholastic India and Macmillan. She participated in the Biennale of Illustrations, Bratislava in 1995.

Taposhi Ghoshal 1966- Ghoshal studied at the College of Art, Delhi and began freelancing in 1993. She has illustrated and designed several children's books, magazines and textbooks. She received the Kalatrayee Award from the Directorate of Education in 1985. Her work has been exhibited in India and abroad.

Tapas Guha 1966- Guha did his post-graduation in Commerce from Delhi. He has been illustrating for children for over a decade.

Ajanta Guhathakurta 1973- Guhathakurta graduated from the College of Art, Delhi. She has illustrated several books and contributed to *Children's World*. She was the Indian nominee for the International Board on Books for Young People Honour List 2002 for her illustrations in the picture-book *Tiger Call*. She is presently working as designer and illustrator with Puffin Books India.

Jagdish Joshi 1937– Joshi has illustrated more than 150 books and won many awards, including the prestigious Noma Concours in 1983 for his picture-book *One Day* (1983). He was nominated for the 1998 Hans Christian Andersen Award for illustration.

Atanu Roy 1950– Illustrator, artist, cartoonist and designer, Roy has illustrated more than 100 books for children and was the Children's Choice Award for book illustrations in 1989. He has won awards at the 1983, 1984, and 1986 Yomiuri Shimbun International Cartoon Contests and contributed to Bob Geldof's *Cartoonaid*, released at the Seoul Olympics. He has worked as an independent art designer in Tokyo and subsequently as a freelance designer and artist. He has his own design studio, ArtGym.

Subir Roy 1954– Roy graduated in Applied Art from Government College of Art, Calcutta. He got a Special Jury mention in BIB, Bratislava for his illustrations in the picture-book *The Woman and the Crow*. He has contributed to the children's magazines *Cricket* and *Cicada* published in the United States. Subir Roy is presently Art Executive with the Children's Book Trust.

Niren Sen Gupta 1940– Sen Gupta studied at Government College of Art, Calcutta and retired as Principal from the College of Art, Delhi, where he taught for more than thirty years. He has illustrated several books for children and has received major awards for his drawings and paintings.

Damayanti Sharma 1968– After graduating from the College of Art, Delhi, Sharma has been illustrating books for several Indian publishers and also regularly contributed to the children's magazine *Cricket*. She has had solo exhibitions of her paintings in 1996, 2000, 2001 and 2002.

Sujata Singh 1962– Singh did a three-year Diploma in Graphic Design and Illustration at Wimbledon School of Art and Design, London. She has worked as a designer and illustrator for *Target, India Today, Business Today, Cosmopolitan, Teens Today, Namaste*, Penguin Books India, Katha, Ratna Sagar, and Kali for Women, among others. She has had several exhibitions of her work in India and abroad.

K.P. Sudesh 1970– Sudesh graduated from the College of Art, Delhi. He has won several awards and has done illustrations for the *Navbharat Times*, Frank Brothers, Vivek Prakashan, Pen Craft Publication, Kohinoor Publication and Penguin Books India.

Bindia Thapar 1957– Thapar has a degree in architecture from the School of Planning and Architecture, Delhi. She has not only illustrated several books for children but also written for them. Her work has been published not only in South Asia, but in England and the United States as well. She is Visiting Faculty at the School of Planning and Architecture, Delhi.